Forward Flash-Back

A Novel

by

G. Owen McGinnis, MD, FACS

HERITAGE BOOKS
2012

HERITAGE BOOKS
AN IMPRINT OF HERITAGE BOOKS, INC.

Books, CDs, and more—Worldwide

For our listing of thousands of titles see our website
at
www.HeritageBooks.com

Published 2012 by
HERITAGE BOOKS, INC.
Publishing Division
100 Railroad Ave. #104
Westminster, Maryland 21157

International Standard Book Numbers
Paperbound: 978-0-7884-5402-8
Clothbound: 978-0-7884-9313-3

Preface

I am old, but remember being young. I am a surgeon, but remember the days before. I know love between a man and woman, but remember when I did not. My life is secure, but I remember when it was not. I have seen struggle and failure and admit it. I have heard odd stories, seen strange wounds and ills in my years. I feel free to write fiction, using memories and emotions from the past.

There is adventure in this story, but primarily it's about enduring love experienced in a strange way and a struggle to regain lost identity. I don't describe the two protagonists in great detail as they appear. At first, the reader will see in a mirror dimly, then face to face enjoy the privilege of discovery. As the reader learns who these people are, the characters discover themselves and try to understand their own changes within and without.

Part One describes the most unlikely way a man and woman might meet and their even stranger courtship. It has a small section of odd physics.

Part Two is a "flash-forward." It stretches the bounds of physiology and problems it causes. A reader is invited to consider what it is like to be officially dead and yet live, denied by family, lost to genealogy, existing as a generic being.

Part One
Curious Encounter

Strange Witness

At the end of a hard day, Job was finishing rounds when he heard the overhead page. He dialed a number on the nearest phone, listened to the message, groaned, and took the elevator down three flights to the GYN clinic. Dr. Goodson was standing in the hall outside the consultation room. He wore a long white coat over his scrub suit like Job. His name was embroidered over the pocket at his chest. Job's coat had a notebook in one lower pocket and a stethoscope in the other, but no name at the top.

Dr. Goodson seemed more anxious than usual as he spoke. "The residents are still in surgery or already gone. I know it's late in the day and unusual to ask, but you'll have to be a witness for this. As you know, two is the number for witness. Come in while I talk with this patient, then I'll check her. She claims assault and injury on her wedding night . . . by her husband. This'll be awkward, but I want you and the nurse there for every word she says . . . and for the examination."

They walked in the consultation room without speaking. Dr. Goodson sat behind the desk and Job sat in a chair to one side. The young patient was sitting in a chair in front of the desk staring straight ahead, alone, with one hand gripping the other--her knuckles white.

The nurse stood when the doctors came in. She wore a white dress with a nametag and gold pen just below it. When the doctors were seated, she held her tiny folded white hat with one hand and sat on the edge of a couch against the wall, but never leaned back. She was trim, but gray hair and sagging cheeks showed years of service.

Dr. Goodson put on dark-rimmed glasses and looked at the chart on his desk. The patient jumped when he spoke. "Mrs. Cain, this is Dr. Ira Jobson. I want him to be a witness to this, since you say there may be legal implications."

She glanced to the side of the desk and said," I don't want some medical student younger than I am staring at that part of my body."

Job reached over, picked up the chart and looked at the cover sheet. "Mrs. Cain, according to your date of birth, in this year of 1955 you're 23. I'm older than you by almost three years. I've finished college and medical school. If you look closer, I have a few gray hairs in the brown. I'm assigned to GYN service this last month of my rotating internship."

Dr. Goodson said, "I'm sure it's embarrassing, but we have to look where the injuries are."

"Then I'm forced to accept a young witness, but don't call me Mrs. Cain. I had to register that way, but I want my old name back. Just call me Lisa."

"You have no family member who could come with you at this difficult time?"

"I have only a guardian . . . the one who arranged my marriage. He would not be appropriate for this and could never have left his business. Maybe I'm in the wrong place. I came here because it was the nearest hospital outside of Birmingham. A woman doctor some other place might be more sympathetic."

Dr. Goodson said, "Look at my wrinkles and white hair. You would be surprised at what I've heard and things I've seen in my years. Tell us why you're here; if at any time you feel uncomfortable, we'll stop."

"Eight days ago, I was married to Amnon Cain . . . not a church wedding, just a civil ceremony. You may find it hard to believe and as I look back I do too, but I hardly knew the man. I had only seen him a few times. We had never had what you would call dates. My guardian arranged it and said this would be a junction of two powerful families. He called me into his office for a long discussion . . . twice. I agreed after the second visit. He told me other countries have arranged marriages. I always thought you married for love, but he said I would learn to love this man. I know every bride is nervous on her wedding night, or at least those without experience are. I even bought a tube of something . . . to make life easier, but he wouldn't use it. He used one of those things men wear . . . in fact he wore two. The outside one was rough. He pushed me on the bed . . . and . . . ." Her words became jumbled and mixed with sobs and tears. The nurse took the few steps, put her arms around Lisa and gave her a tissue.

Dr. Goodson said, "Take your time. When you are ready, begin again."

"He almost smothered me and . . . I don't know what else to call it . . . he began moving and hurting me. Something happened . . . a sort of jerking and he stopped. He stormed out of the room saying I was not capable of . . . of intimacy, but he used another word. He told me I would have to have an operation. He didn't come close to me until six days later. The second attempt was the same, but worse. After this episode, he told me he was leaving for South America the next day for work in my guardian's business. He said I was his property and he wanted my surgery done before he got back. That was two days ago. I began to realize what I had done. I had a hard time remembering everything about the second visit when I agreed to the marriage. I might have lied to your secretary when I told her it was an emergency. In a way it is; I have to go back to work tomorrow. "

The nurse led Lisa into the exanimation room with the glaring lights and frightening smells. The nurse held the shielding sheet and Lisa removed her lower clothing and lay on the table. The nurse elevated Lisa's legs in stirrups and draped her for pelvic exam. The nurse could not help staring and now she had tears. She called the doctors in. Job stood, said nothing, looked over Dr. Goodson's shoulder as he sat on the stool and lifted the towel covering the pubic area. There were bruises and swellings around the entire exposed area. One small tear was covered with a crust and circled red. Dr. Goodson explained everything as the gentle exam took place.

The nurse said, "Doctor, there is a place under the drapes you need to see." She pulled them back to show an abrasion around the thigh.

Lisa said, "He tore off my underclothes."

"Then we need to check the upper area."

"No, he never bothered them."

After Lisa dressed and dried her tears, they all sat in the consultation room again. Dr. Goodson began. "Now uh . . . Miss Lisa, you didn't want photographs so I will make my records very thorough. I know your injuries are painful and frightening. Please be assured that within the month, you will be healed and clear . . . physically, but not emotionally. I can also certify that you have never had true sexual relations. Your marriage was never consummated."

Lisa clutched one hand then the other and said, "But is it possible what he said might be true? Must I have an operation to be able to perform a . . . a natural function?"

"At this time, I don't want to brutalize you further and tear tissues with a large speculum. That would only add to your pain. I see nothing abnormal, but with the swelling, I can't be certain with the superficial exam. I cannot answer that question. Your husband may need counseling."

"I don't want to think of him as my husband. I came to learn of any permanent damage and of my future. You have answered my first question, but I hear uncertainty about the other. I desperately need to know what life holds for me." She stood and turned to leave.

The nurse walked with Lisa to the door. She squeezed her arm and said, "I don't know what to say except it's not supposed to be like that. An act of love shouldn't be filled with terror. I will pray for your recovery . . . your emotional recovery."

* * *

Several weeks later, Job answered an outside call. The voice said. "This is J. D. Bildad, I am attorney for Lisa Cain. I have what I believe to be an emergency situation. I am calling you because I was told Dr. Goodson had a heart attack and died last week. I am preparing an appeal for a marriage annulment for Mrs. Cain. My client got a letter she thinks may be contaminated. She is still scrubbing her hands. Can the letter be sterilized and still be legible as evidence and can you arrange it? It may not be necessary, but she thinks it is. You probably want to check her records. Call me back as soon as you can."

Job said, "I don't need the chart. Some patients are never forgotten. I can't leave the surgical clinic. Wrap it in something and bring it to our ER. I'll look at it when I can. If I think it'll survive steam sterilization, I'll ask the OR to do it."

"I'll be there in 20 minutes. One more thing . . . since Goodson has died, I want you to testify about my client's office visit. Before the case comes up, I'll talk with you more."

Job unwrapped the package enough to see the dark pencil lines before he had the letter sterilized. He picked it up in the OR too late in the afternoon to call the lawyer and stuffed it in the pocket of his white coat. After he ate, he went to his room in the house-staff quarters, sat on his bed, unwrapped the envelope and stared at it several minutes. *I shouldn't read a love letter, but from what I heard at her visit, it's probably not a love letter. If I am to testify, I need to know all I can.* He took out the single wrinkled sheet and read. There was no salutation; words began in a heavy pencil scrawl—some places leaving dents in the paper. "I hope to be back in two months. My father is here to help now. That should give plenty time to get over your operation. I am getting some practice with local women so that should help. Might take longer than two months. I don't think it's a venereal disease; it's just in a bad place. They say it's the yaws. Slow for the shots to fix and it comes back." No "with love" or even "yours truly," just "Amnon Cain." Job put the page back in the envelope, wrapped it with the OR cloth, went to the bathroom and washed his hands. He knew the letter was sterile, but he felt dirty.

When Job delivered the letter to the attorney, they went over his testimony.

Strange Trial

Job heard nothing until he was called weeks later as a witness for the petition for a marriage annulment. In the courtroom, Lisa gave her teary testimony. Mr. Cain was still in South America, but contested the procedure. His lawyer asked little of a woman in tears.

Job took the witness stand. He read Goodson's notes from the chart describing the reason for Lisa's visit, her physical findings, and then added his own observations.

The defense attorney took the chart from Job. He began with a pleasant voice and smile. "Dr. Jobson, I see you also signed this record as a witness. You have said you are now a surgical resident, but you were an intern on GYN at the time of Mrs. Cain's visit. You were there for the entire office visit?"

"Yes."

"You have referred to the chart and told us she had bruises and swelling of the . . . the entire pubic area."

"Yes."

"Did you feel this with your own hands and if not how can you be sure of the findings?"

"As a physician and surgeon, I am a trained observer. I saw the injuries from two feet. I could have recognized them from across the room."

The attorney nodded and said, "It's all well and good to talk about what happens between a man and a women, but what do you know from personal experience, or do you just read about it?" Now he did not smile.

Mr. Bildad said, "Objection, Dr. Jobson's personal life should not be part of these proceedings."

"We need to know about the qualifications of this witness. He has been presented as an expert witness . . . a physician. Now he can tell us if he speaks from book knowledge only. I think that is a reasonable question to ask."

The judge said, "I will allow the witness to briefly answer that one question, but do not pursue the matter."

The room was quiet and everybody looked at Job. "One year ago, my wife of one month was killed by a drunk driver. That is my total personal experience beyond books."

"No further questions."

With the history of physical and verbal abuse and testimony that consummation had never taken place, annulment was granted. Lisa, Mr. Bildad and Job left the courtroom and walked down the steps to the parking lot. They stopped to talk by a grassy strip at the base of the building. They stepped around mud spilled over from holes dug for new shrubbery, but abandoned because of heavy rain in the night. In the late afternoon there were only scattered cars left in the lot. As they talked, Job saw motion to one side and turned to see a man getting out of his car, leaving the door open. He took a few steps toward them, stopped, pulled a pistol from his belt and held it up with both hands. When Job heard the cocking sound, he jumped and knocked Lisa against her attorney. As the gun fired, Job felt a burning jolt to his shoulder, heard the smack of the bullet on the wall, and fell in the shrubbery mud hole. He lifted his face out of the water and heard three more shots. The attorney pulled him out of the mud. When he was upright, Job saw the man with the gun lying on the ground. A deputy coming out the building just behind them was sitting on the pavement holding his side.

Job struggled to stand and said, "Mr. Bildad, please go inside and call for help. I need to check that deputy. "

"But you're shot, too. There's blood on your back."

"I can breathe okay; I hope it's not deep." He took a few stumbling steps to the wounded man. The deputy was bleeding from a left upper abdominal wound. Job told Lisa, "Find something to put under his head and let him lie down. Put a little pressure on the wound. I'll look at the shooter." Within minutes, police cars and ambulances surrounded them. The deputy left first. The shooter was dead from shots to the chest, but he had to be taken to a hospital to make it official. The third ambulance brought a stretcher for Job, although he told them he had rather sit for what he knew to be a rough ride.

"And where are you taking me . . . a car-wash?"

He heard what he expected and said, "No, take me to Lloyd Noland."

"That's farther out—not even in Birmingham."

"I'm not that critical and besides, I work there." Job did lie on the stretcher in a pool of muddy water on a white sheet. As they were about to close the back doors, Lisa said, "Could I ride too, so I know where he's going?"

"Are you family?"

"Well . . . no."

"Only family goes."

"Then yes, I'm family."

"Sorry, we go by the first answer." Lisa watched as the ambulance pulled away.

The ER doctor took a quick look at Job's wound and said, "That's not too bad. A tetanus shot, a good bath, a little salve and it'll be fine."

In the ambulance, Job had wiped the mud off the left hand and felt the wound. He said, "Please call a surgical resident."

The resident agreed with Job, and under local anesthesia scrubbed the wound, explored it, cut away a few cloth fibers, then a small bone chip. He excised the edges and loosely closed the short wound in the back of the shoulder. Job did get the tetanus shot and a penicillin shot. As he finished, the resident said, "I hate to see you try to put on those muddy clothes. You have one gown covering the front side, what if we put another on your backside? I see your clothes all wrapped up mud and all. I taped a piece of rubber sheeting over the dressing so you can shower, if you can get to one. I would take you to the quarters, but I have to work tonight."

Lisa was standing at the door and heard his words. "I'll take him. It's the least I can do. He may not have told you, but he saved my life."

Job put on his second gown, got another wrap for his muddy clothes and one to protect the car seat.

Stranger Outcome
After they drove several bocks, Job said, "I told you where they were. This is an odd way to the house-staff quarters . . . or the courthouse parking lot if you're taking me to my car."

"You took the bullet and fell in that mud hole to save my life. Your muddy shirt and pants look like cotton. I have a washer at my house. While you shower, I will wash your clothes. I used to do my dad's things. There's a gas heater in the utility room. Your things should dry fast in front of that. How's your shoulder?"

"After I got the treatment I asked for, it's fine. Now that the Novocain is wearing off, it only hurts if I hold my arm straight up, but I can do without that for a few days. What will your neighbors think when you bring home a man in a gown? They're probably all at home at this time of day."

"I'll unlock the door first, then you get out of the car and walk the few steps to the house. It'll just take a second or two. Besides, I don't care. This is one of my guardian's houses. He has me move every few months; I've done that since my mother died. Are you sure your shoulder doesn't hurt when you move?"

"Only when I try to play Statue of Liberty."

They parked in the garage and walked through the side door into a utility room. Lisa put his bundle of muddy clothes on the washer. "I'm sure you are starving. Come in the kitchen; there are some cookies to tide you over 'til you clean up."

She waited while he ate and then showed him to the bathroom. "I guess you want to take those cloth gowns back to the hospital. Before you get in the shower, throw them out in the hall and I'll put them in the washer. Here is a brand new toothbrush. I'm sure you want to brush the cookies out."

Job said, "You haven't been running. You seem so short of breath."

"I'm fine. Just throw all those things out so I can wash them; I'll bring your clothes back when they're dry."

Job soaked in the shower and scrubbed off the dried mud that was even caked in his hair. He stepped out of the shower, dried, peeled the waterproof strip off his bandage, wrapped a towel around his middle, stood at the sink and used the new toothbrush. He took a gulp of mouthwash, rinsed, bent over the sink to empty the wash and ran water to clean the sink. With all the noise, he didn't hear the door ease open. As he dried his face with the hand towel, he felt something soft against his arm. He put down the towel and turned to see Lisa. Her wrap-around outer garment was hardly a shadow. He couldn't help looking down. Two scanty strips were under the shadow. She was taking short jerking breaths.

After moments of silence, Lisa said, "I didn't know about your wife. I am sorry for your loss. I know no other can be her . . . but as a woman, I think she wouldn't want your life to end when hers did." Now Job had trouble breathing and could say nothing. Lisa said, "This is awkward for me. I've never even spoken your first name."

He stammered the words, "It's Ira . . . but I'm usually called Job."

More silence—then Lisa said, "This outfit is not a leftover. I bought it today when I got your toothbrush. I knew the hospital you went to, but I almost didn't make it to the ER before they finished your treatment." She turned her head to one side and looked up. "Am I not attractive to you at all? I showered in the other bath and would have used perfume, but it's in here."

Job took a deep breath and said, "You are beautiful and attractive from the top hair of your head to the soles of your feet and have your own perfume, but do you do this only in gratitude?"

"I am grateful for my life. You took the shot meant for me. You were the witness for my annulment, but now I ask for something else. You know what that beast told me about surgery. The fear that what he said might be true has tortured me. Your Dr. Goodson couldn't totally reassure me. I did heal like he promised, but I have to know if I should resign myself to living alone the rest of my life . . . or am I normal. I believe you to be a kind man . . . and gentle."

Job put his arms around the shadow garment and bent down—not far—she was tall.

Lisa trembled and pulled away. "I've never been kissed like that before. It's so . . . so. . . ."

". . . so intimate. Yes, I meant it as a serious kiss." He held his towel with one hand and her hand with the other and they walked down the hall.

In the light of early morning, Job woke to hear faint noises from the kitchen. He sat up and saw the pillow blocking him from the other side of the bed. That side was empty. He still had nothing but his towel. He found his washed and dried clothes in the bathroom. The hole in his shirt was trimmed and sewn with a slight pucker. His toothbrush was where he left it. He washed his face, but couldn't shave. He said "Good morning" as he entered the kitchen and sat at the table. Lisa gave a weak reply and was silent as she put down the food. They said nothing as they ate.

Job finished and stared across the table. Lisa looked up with a frown and said, "I hope you're not one to talk and brag. At the end of that ordeal at the courthouse, I suddenly wanted to know the rest of my future . . . I had to know. On impulse, I did seduce you last night. I can't believe I did it. If I had taken time to think about it and plan it, I would never have done it. We're mot married. We shouldn't have. This episode ends now. I have no deformities. I was just forced to accept a crude husband. I can't believe I did it, but we have proved that I am capable of . . . of intimate . . . uh . . . events."

Job smiled. "Yes, twice."

"I didn't expect the second. It wasn't necessary. I should have moved to the couch."

"Remember what Goodson said; two is the number of witness. Besides, you seemed to get with the program more the second time. I don't want everything to end.

Do you remember what I told you last night . . . more than once?"

"That was something said in the heat of passion . . . nothing more."

"When you unloaded my coat last night, I hope you saved a little thin notebook. Do you remember the day you came to the clinic at our hospital . . . the first day I ever saw you? Turn to a page with that date and tell me what you see."

She picked up the book in the utility room, sat at the table again, flipped pages and stopped to check dates at the top. "Some are water soaked and hard to read. Oh, here it is . . . down on this page is my name, phone number and where I used to live. Why is this here?"

"You legally belonged to another so I never called, but I wanted to."

"But why? We were nothing to each other. I never saw you before that day at the hospital."

"Your guardian is wrong. I've had a long time to think this through. Love between a man and woman is not a skill or trade to be learned like carpentry or plumbing while lust binds them together. Some would say love is a strong affection or emotion, but it's more. Without invitation or effort, it begins deep within, rises, consumes and holds. Love dominates thoughts and actions. It's not earned, but discovered and realized. A man or woman may learn to demonstrate and fulfill that love . . . but it's already there within. It could be shown by rings and pearls, but most times it's through objects of little monetary value and things one does for the other or says to the other—a sudden extended hand or a certain look. Whether involved or trivial, the other clearly sees these as signs of love. Some know love at first encounter. Some recognize it slowly. Others see it too late, when all opportunity is gone. Love may defy logic. Love is strong. It endures tragedy and strife. Once realized, true love is everlasting."

Job stopped, but began again before Lisa could answer. "Let me tell you in the light of day. I thought I could never love another. I did see you in that exam room and felt more than compassion. Remember, I first saw you and heard your words of disappointment and grief across Goodson's desk. Before I saw your wounds, I heard the voice and saw the person within. I think I loved you that minute, but I couldn't admit it to myself. In the weeks to come, at the end of a long day, I sat in my empty room and stared at your name in that book enough times to know it was true. I looked up the meaning of your name. Lisa means *a gift from God*. I did love you in the heat of passion last night, but I loved before . . . and I love now in the light of day. After the annulment yesterday, you are free and I can say the words."

Lisa frowned and said, "My guardian told me love can be learned, that a husband should be chosen from the proper background and family."

"Is that your guardian's picture on that wall?"

"Yes, he wants me to look at it when he calls. He asks me if I am looking at it every time. He says it makes me feel closer to him."

"I am surprised he hasn't called. He must have known about the annulment proceedings."

"I took the phone off the hook last night."

Job stood and looked at the life-sized portrait. The face almost filled the frame. Lighting in the photograph seemed to make a glow around his face. The eyes were black, piercing and seemed to follow as Job moved around the room. He pulled the picture away from the wall, twisted the long cords and put it back facing the wall. "When he calls, tell him you are looking at his picture. You don't have to say it's the back. If he should ask, say you haven't touched it. If he tries to talk about the annulment or some other thing you don't want to hear, think about washing dishes or scrubbing the floor and don't listen to his every word. From what you tell me, he directs major events in your life. "

He sat down and looked into Lisa's eyes. "I will go now. Thank you for washing my clothes, giving me shelter for the night and most of all, a chance for me to show my love. I have told you how I feel; I will not push the issue."

He still looked at Lisa and showed a slight smile. "Can we date?"

"What! You mean come here once a week and jump in bed?"

"Oh no, just a regular date-date: movies, dinner, that sort of thing. I have tried to understand your act of desperation last night and will not use that as a standard. In our dates, I will not cross the threshold of your front door. I will not touch you without permission. There is a new girlie-type movie at the Alabama. I see by your morning paper, the feature should start a little after seven. I'll pick you up tonight about half past six. We can see the movie, the newsreel, maybe a cartoon and listen to the organ." He wrote on a note pad and pushed it across the table. "Here is my number. Call me if you get a better offer for the evening."

Lisa stared with open mouth as the front door closed. She looked at the wall with the picture several minutes, then jumped up, ran around searching for car keys, found the keys, ran to the car, and then back to lock the door of the house. She backed the car out, and pulled around the corner with a sight screech of tires. She drove around several blocks before she found Job. She stopped at the curb and rolled down the window. "And just where are you going?"

"I think there is a bus line, a block or so over; if not, I'll walk to the lot."

"I am truly sorry. Get in; I forgot you were on foot."

They didn't speak until she turned into the lot. Job said, "There 's my car. They may have thought it wasn't worth towing." As he got out, he said, "Thank you for the ride."

Before he closed the door Lisa said, "You were serious about tonight?"

"I told you, unless you call, I will be there at half past six." She waited to be sure his car would start before she left.

* * *

That evening, Job parked his car and knocked on Lisa's door. She opened almost immediately. He said, "I am a few minutes early. Traffic wasn't as heavy as I expected. I'll wait in the car, if you're not ready. I hope you won't be ashamed to ride in my old car. It runs better than it looks."

Lisa was ready; they left and got to the movie early enough for center seats. As the feature began, Job leaned toward Lisa and whispered, "May I hold your hand?" She hesitantly moved her hand and Job grabbed it. At an especially emotional scene in the movie, she squeezed his hand. He squeezed back. She glanced at him and made a limp attempt to pull away. Job held tighter and whispered, "You said it was okay. I can pretend the squeeze was for me."

Conversation began to increase on the way home. They parked in front of Lisa's house and talked. Job said, "I'm working next weekend. My hours at the hospital are long. I can't go out weekdays, but I'll call you. Unlike when you talk to your guardian, I don't need a picture; I see your face when I hear your voice. Could we have a church date tomorrow? You do go to church don't you?"

"After last night, we should go to church?"

"Churches are for sinners not saints. Where do you go to church?"

"First Church, right downtown. I haven't been in a while. It's hard to go alone."

"Fine; I'll be here in time to make the service. There is a little Chinese restaurant close by that I can afford for lunch. We can drive your car if you like. Mine will look crummy in the church parking lot."

Job walked her to the door, said goodnight while she was unlocking, turned and left before she went in.

* * *

Job was early again. They did drive Lisa's car. They left it in the parking lot after church and ate at the Chinese restaurant. Words and smiles flowed freely so they walked to a park and sat on a bench to talk.

Job reached for Lisa's hand--her eyes seemed to say yes. "Did your guardian call?"

"Less than an hour after I hung up the phone after you left. He said I would have to remarry that man. I did what you suggested and it seemed to help. He wanted me to come in to talk. I made excuses. Then the sheriff called. The man who shot you had five hundred dollars and a picture of me in his pocket. The sheriff brought the photo by for me to identify. Mother made an album for me before she died. I had added a picture made a few months ago on the last page. That space in the album was empty. He said the dead man was known to be a paid assassin and always worked alone. I did something I have rarely done; I called my guardian . . . just a few hours after he called me. I told him again what happened, then what I was told about the shooter, and what I suspected. He said he would take care of it . . . whatever that means."

Job said, "I don't understand why you have a guardian at your age. You're old enough to make your own decisions."

"He has testamentary guardianship . . . I suppose forever. My mother and dad died in the same year. I am an only child. My guardian produced a will giving him control of my inheritance and my life. It says I am incompetent. He furnishes me with a car, house and job. I have no idea how my dad's business is doing. I have asked, but he says that is his responsibility and a young girl wouldn't understand."

"Then you are a legal prisoner. Your life is not your own." Job looked at the lengthening shadows and said, "We better take you hone before they haul away your car. I have an early case in the morning. I need to get some sleep, if I can sleep."

At Lisa's front door, Job said. "I tell you again, as junior surgical resident, I work long hours and I have to stay in the hospital when I'm on call. I probably can't see you in person for two weeks, but I will call." He turned to leave.

She said, "Wait. If we are to date, promise me you will forget how we met . . . and . . . and what happened Friday night. It was my fault. I wish I hadn't done it. I'm not that kind of person."

Job looked back to see Lisa near tears. He resisted the temptation to touch her and said, "I know your hospital visit is important for you to forget. I'll try, but Friday night is another story. For me, it was a sudden unexpected way to show my feelings. I have promised to not pursue the matter. I can't forget a time of joy, but I'll promise to never tell others, gloat over it, or remind you of it." He turned again and went down the walk. She stood in the doorway and watched him drive away.

Life Goes On

They lived for dates every two weeks and weekday phone calls for months. As they walked to Lisa's front door one Saturday night, she said, "This house is very old, but new to me. It's a warm night. I've never had a porch since I was a little girl. Could we sit in the swing and talk for a while? I know you can't use names, but surely in the last two weeks you have seen something weird or wonderful in the hospital. The movie wasn't much to talk about. I can tell you what I know about this old house."

As they sat, a car turned the corner and headlights swept across the porch. As the light hit them, Job turned away toward the big single pane window by the swing. The ancient glass had a wavy area and bubbles in the center. As the light moved across, it seemed to give a sense of motion--or did something really move behind the glass. After the car passed, Job jerked around and interrupted Lisa's words about her new-old house. "Who besides you has a key to this house?"

"Nobody does. After somebody took that photograph from the album, each time I have to move, I ask that I have the only set of keys."

"Don't show any change; keep talking and smiling, but listen to me. There is a man in your house. I saw his face through the window for a second, when that car made the turn. I'll go next door and ask them to call the police." In spite of the warming, Lisa showed a look of horror. Job squeezed her hand. "Remember to smile. It's dark in the house; we can't see him, but he may be watching us."

Lisa said, "Let me go. I just met the neighbor next-door today. She said call her if she could help in any way."

"I'll be watching you. Go ask her to call, but don't go in her house;. Come back and we sit and talk or pretend to talk, 'til the cops come. Tell them no sirens, if they want to catch somebody."

Police arrived in an unmarked car. Two officers got out. As they came up the walk, one complained about "another woman scared of shadows." Lisa unlocked the door and both men went in.

Job said, "Shouldn't one of you cover the back door? This was not a shadow. I saw him."

One officer snorted and said, "We go together. If the shadows are real, there might be two."

Job ran to the back. Within a minute, he heard the door unlocked, opened and a man ran out. Job squatted by the steps and raised a rake handle. The man caught his ankles on it, flew through the air and landed face down in the grass. He lay stunned with feeble movements of his arms and legs. Job shouted for help. The man was near to Job's height of just under six-feet, but was thicker. Job held the rake to be ready. The man was getting up when the police came through the house. His face was coarse, angry, and grass stained. He began shouting, "This is my wife's house. I have every right to be here." Lisa screamed when she saw him.

One officer said, "Miss, is what he says true?"

"He was my husband, but the marriage was annulled. He is not my husband now and has broken into my house."

"We didn't see evidence of forced entry. He must have had a key."

"Please take him away. He has some kind of terrible disease. I don't want him even near me" The officers loaded him in their car and left.

Job forgot his promise about touching and held Lisa until she stopped crying. "Now where will I go? I will not stay in that house. I won't even go in the house. Look, all the neighbors are out and staring. I couldn't live in this neighborhood anyway."

Job said, "My folks live out of town. There is no place for women at the hospital, except as a patient. I guess I could admit you."

"No, you might get in trouble. I have a checkbook in my purse. I can go to a hotel for the night and call my guardian in the morning. I don't think I could hold myself together long enough to talk tonight, even if I could reach him. Could you drive me?"

At the registration desk the clerk said, "Is the gentleman registering also? And . . . no luggage?"

"Her house has been damaged and is not habitable."

"I see. Will you stay more than one night . . . or less?"

"I'll walk her to the room and leave. If she can arrange for housing, she will be gone by checkout time tomorrow."

In the room, Job held Lisa while she shed more tears. Between sobs she said, "I thought I saw a face in the window, but it was there less than a second and gone when the car passed. I've seen that face in nightmares. I thought it was my imagination. I would have died if he had come after me in that house. You have saved me again."

"Do you want me to stay the night? I could sleep on a rollaway or even on the floor."

"No, you need to go. I can't sleep in this dress. Something might happen. Temptation might be too much. I know we have, but you know we shouldn't. We drove my car; just keep it for the night. Be sure to wave at the clerk when you leave. Call me in the morning. We have to do something about your car in front of that house."

The next morning, Job made several attempts on the phone before he heard Lisa's voice. She said, "I have a different house, but smaller. The key was left at the desk. I have nothing to wear so we have to skip our Sunday date. I called a cousin who works weekends at the jail. When Amnon got there, he must have called my guardian and not a lawyer. He got out on bond a few hours later. My cousin was standing outside the door when he left. A man gave him money and told the taxi driver to take them to the airport . . . the private side.

I hate to ask, but please go through every foot of the new house before I go in. One more thing I ask you to do: go through the house I was living in and take out all my things. I move so often, I don't have many. I want you to wear a gown and gloves like you were in the operating room. I don't want you catching anything."

"Lisa, yaws happens in hot high humidity places. I don't think it's a problem here."

"I want them out anyway."

"And do what with your clothes?"

"Burn everything. I will be late for work, but I'll buy something new. I don't want to wear anything that man has touched or been around."

He borrowed a gown, mask, and gloves from the OR and they drove first to her new small house. Lisa waited in the car while Job went through the house. Furniture was old and worn, but reasonably clean. He checked every room and closet, then walked Lisa through.

They drove both cars to the house with the porch. Lisa waited in her car again while Job went in. Her under things were in disarray, as if somebody had been through them. Two were torn. In a separate spot he found the shadow garment and the two strips, neatly folded. He hesitated, and then put them in a paper bag with the others. He took shoes out of boxes and loaded them in bags. He put her jewelry in a smaller bag. He put the album and what he thought were family items in another bag. Job emptied drawers, took down clothes on hangers and carried them to the porch. At one end of her closet he found an outfit he had never seen. Job suddenly realized that it was low cut and would show a lot of neck and shoulder skin. He carried the bags to the porch and locked the door. He piled the bags and the closet contents on the back seat of his car. He took off the gown, gloves, mask and hat and put them in a hospital bag. Job stopped at Lisa's car. "I will take your under things to the hospital incinerator. I can understand not wanting them next to your skin. I see no reason to throw away your outer clothes. I'll take them to be cleaned or washed. Our clothes are cleaned with those from diseased people all the time. Chemicals and enough water take care of the problem. You'll have a big cleaning and laundry bill, but less than one for all new clothes. I will soak jewelry in a solution to sterilize. If you can't make yourself wear them, you could sell them. I'll wipe down your shoes and the album with a solution. Are you okay to drive?" She nodded. "Call me when your phone is hooked up." Neighbors were staring again.

Suddenly Serious
They again lived for time together every two weeks and visits on the phone. Lisa insisted on paying for meals some days. She warned against expensive gifts for her, but bought things for him. She told Job she made far more than he did. One Saturday night, they stopped to talk after Lisa unlocked her door. There was no porch on her small house. Words stopped. In the moonlight, they looked at each other in silence and it seemed to Job that Lisa wanted to say something, but couldn't.

In the stillness, Job whispered, "May I kiss you goodnight?"

"Yes . . . but nothing serious."

He leaned down and put his arms around her. Within seconds, she pulled him tight and made it serious. She then whirled and slammed the door. He heard her running down the hall, but knocked on the door anyway. She didn't answer.

He drove back to his quarters. The phone was ringing when he walked up the steps. Between sobs Lisa said, "It's all my fault. I'm sorry I slammed the door. I didn't want to make it serious, it just happened. I was afraid of what might come next, and you know we shouldn't."

After Lisa's voice became more even, Job said, "I think it's time we had a serious talk. I didn't plan for it to be on the phone, but let's try. Long ago, I told you how I feel."

Lisa interrupted, "I know you haven't said the words again. You promised you wouldn't. Our time together and things you have done for me speak louder than words. I have practiced for weeks, but I couldn't tell you. I couldn't get the words out. That's why I ran away. In the last month, I have realized how much I love you. I think I have since . . . since that Friday or I couldn't have done what I did that night. I knew that day you would risk your life for me and took the shot meant for me. My feelings for you were sudden and different."

Job said, "Beyond my love, I like you. You are my best friend. I can't conceive of life without you."

After seconds of silence, Lisa said, "Am I to consider this to be a telephone proposal?"

"I didn't plan it this way, it just happened like that serious kiss."

"I would accept even if the words came by carrier pigeon."

"Then we need to do some face-to-face talking. Tomorrow after church and lunch, we can sit in your car."

The next day, they parked at Lisa's house. Job said, "We must face facts, I don't make enough as Junior-Resident to support a wife. A hundred dollars a month doesn't go far. When I make Chief-Resident, my check will be enough to support us . . . but barely."

Lisa said, "I'm working; we should have enough now."

"But isn't your job at the whim of your guardian? And he said you have to marry that other guy . . . the face in the window."

Lisa said, "We need to talk to my guardian and explain. I work in the same building, but he is isolated from employs. We'll have to get an appointment. He claims to be interested in my future. I haven't seen him in person in a long time . . . probably not since he convinced me to marry Amnon. You should be able to communicate with him better than I can. He is a doctor, too . . . or was until he got into all these businesses."

"Don't tell me he's a psychiatrist."

"I think they called him a psychoanalyst."

"And a hypnotherapist?"

"I think so."

"And he took over businesses of his patients?"

"I know of some he did. He took over my dad's after he and my mother died."

"I hate to ask, but how did they die?"

"There was an explosion in my dad's plant. About three months later, my mother and her sister, who was my guardian's wife, went to the coast and out into a storm in the Gulf. Others tried to talk them out of the trip, but the ship captain said it was my guardian's boat and he told him in person to show the women the storm. They never came back. I now have no close relatives left."

"You have just explained your strange circumstances. Think about your few visits to your guardian . . . your uncle-in-law. He sits a little above you with a light on his face while you are in the dark?"

"Not totally dark, but dim light, and he wants you to look in his eyes while he talks in this monotone voice."

"Think hard. What else do you remember?"

"There is some kind of strange soft sound and even stranger smell. I'm not sure, but it seems to come from the floor and rise in a mist. The sound seems to come from all around. I'm frightened at first, but then seem to relax."

"He controls your inheritance and your life. We can talk to him, but I have to think of something to fight his total domination of senses."

* * *

On Saturday afternoon two weeks later, they sat in Lisa's car parked by a stone building with a single door and no windows—not veneer walls, but rectangular blocks of stone. A stack of stones on the sides shielded the door on the far right. Lisa said there was a door almost the same at the back for employees. She made trips through it every workday. A small sign above the door read, "Crunchner International." Job said, "Before we get out, let's make our plans. We can't protect all sensory stimulation and messages we don't want to hear, but let's try this. I stuff your ears with cotton and stain it a little on the outside so the white doesn't shine. We stuff your nose with cotton and you wear these dark glasses. I'll do the same."

"But these glasses are so dark, I can hardly see."

"That's the idea. He can't see where you're looking. Turn your face toward him, but your eyes to the side. Don't look at him when he talks-- especially his eyes. We tell him we both have severe conjunctivitis and can't stand light. I have a bottle of eye drops we can show. Your voice will be a little changed, but that will go along with our supposed illness. Put one of these cough drops in your mouth before we go in. Don't roll it around or he will know something is on your tongue. You have worn long sleeves, long skirt, and thick stockings as I asked you to. Hold your clothes as close as you can. I don't know of anything else we can do against something absorbed through the skin. Don't listen to what he says. The cotton will soften his words a little. Think about something else or count backward in your mind and say 'yes' or 'I understand' when it seems right. If we can sit close, I will nudge you when you need to say something."

"Our appointment is at three, we better go."

They rang the bell and looked toward the camera. The steel door slid open. Lisa spoke to the man at the desk. He did a pat-down search on Job and called a woman from the down the hall to check Lisa. They were ushered into a small room—empty but for two chairs. They sat in the chairs fixed to the floor two feet apart. The wall in front had a three-foot opening into darkness. The other walls were bare. The lights slowly dimmed and a faint circle of light shone on them. In front, a light appeared in the dark square, became brighter and began to glow around a face.

"Lisa, why do you come? It is not a workday for you, Why do you bring a stranger? Remove those glasses so I may see your face."

"Pardon me for interrupting, sir. I am a doctor in residency. We both have severe conjunctivitis. If we took off the glasses, we couldn't open our eyes. We even have to use our eye drops in a darkened room."

After what seemed a full minute, the face in the light said, "Very well, just look directly at me when I speak so I know you hear my words."

Even with the cotton plugs, Job heard the strange sound and faintly smelled the rising mist.

Lisa explained their feelings for each other and their wish to be married. She asked his permission and his assurance of her house and job.

"You have frivolous ideas. I know what is best. You must remarry Amnon Cain. He is the one I have chosen for you. The families must be joined. You will learn to care for him." He began a long string of monotonous words.

Job coughed.

"Silence when I speak or leave the room. I wish to talk to you, but I will choose the time." The voice in the light then told Lisa she could not marry Job and even to ask again would cost her house, car, and job. He then told Job he was a nobody with nothing to offer and to get out of Lisa's life or he would live to regret it.

The glowing face slowly disappeared and the overhead lights came on. Job stood, but Lisa sat staring at darkness where the face had been. The door behind then opened and the man at the desk said, "The visit with Dr. Crunchner is now over."

Job took Lisa's hand, pulled her to a standing position, and led her across the waiting room to the hall. He turned her around and took off her glasses. Her eyes were dull and she had no expression. He pulled her close, kissed her, and then shook her. She began to breath harder, jerked, and pulled away. Now there was life in her eyes. She said, "Please take me away from this place." They didn't speak during the drive home.

After he parked, Job said, "How much do you remember and how much did he get to you?"

"I was okay until the very end when he told me those terrible things about you. I must have looked and been wrapped up in whatever he does to people."

"So what do you think? Are you willing to throw everything away for a nobody like me with only three coats and one of those with a patch on the shoulder?"

"I would give away ten of everything I have and more. I have fulfilled my obligation to that evil man. I never want to see him again. I'm sorry you had to had to endure this visit. We might be able to work out the finances some way. Don't we need to talk to your parents?"

"We can do that tomorrow if they are at home and if you can stand another confrontation in the same weekend."

* * *

They spoke little during the 50-mile drive the next morning. They stopped at his parents' house at the edge of town. Job hesitated at the door he had opened so many times in the past and then knocked. His father opened almost immediately. His mother was sitting in a chair near the door, but got up and took a few steps.

Greetings were restrained and solemn. They sat in the living room Job remembered as a formal room for company.

Job began, "I told you it was an urgent matter we wanted to speak about." He then told of their love and great wish to be married. He said, "I know you sent me to college and medical school. After that, you have helped me with the old car and a little money now and then. I am grateful for all that. I know at times it was a sacrifice with your income. I would not do anything so major as marriage without telling you and asking your blessings."

Lisa said, "Let me say something at the very beginning. If love and devotion mean anything, I will be a good wife to your son."

His father never looked at Lisa, but stared at Job with an almost sour face and said, "You have been a major expense and at times a burden for eight years and even now we help you some. You are years away from earning a decent living. You married once before and your wife died in a month. You should have seen that as a sign and finish your training before you have a family."

Job stood slowly as if under a great burden. He didn't ball his fist, but bent his fingers into his palms and straightened them slowly several times and took deep jerking breaths as he struggled for words. "God is not a demon who takes the life of an innocent person to punish another guilty only of love. You make it difficult to honor the first commandment with a promise. Thank you for all you have done for me and opportunities you have opened for me. I will always be grateful for my education. I have my answer. This visit is over. In the time to come, I will ask for nothing more." His mother was trying to say something about staying for lunch as they went out the door. Job didn't look back or try to answer.

Job sat in the car, closed the door, put his head down on the steering wheel and said, "I thought we should tell them. I'm sorry; it was worse than I expected or could imagine."

Lisa said, "Do you want me to drive?"

"Yes, it would be much safer."

At Lisa's house, they sat in the car in silence for several minutes. Job said, "The only good thing about this weekend is that I got to see you. Do all the angry words we heard change your mind?"

"No, and neither will others, even if it's just you and me against the world. I don't see it now, but we'll find a way."

"I just wanted to hear you say it. I'll see you in two weeks. I'll call tomorrow."

* * * * * * * *

Far South

Amnon and his father David shouted at their men, "I saw you light it, saw it burn, but nothing's happening. You stupid clumsy excuses for workers have pulled the fuse out of the charge again." They were angrier by having to think of Spanish and Indian words to condemn the men. They were walking down the slope toward the charge when the blast went off. Each was thrown up the hill and landed on his back.

Workers gathered around them. "Look, they do not move, they do not speak, yet they breathe. I see nothing broken. They still live. What do we do?"

Another said, "They are evil men. When we fall, they do not help us. They make us work like slaves; they take our women. They pay us little. Let them lie."

Another said, "In this sun, they will die soon. We need a priest to tell us what to do."

"There is no priest within hours. Go bring Jesus."

"Which one?"

"Jesus Martinez, he is the oldest and wisest in our town."

Twenty minutes later, a man with white hair and beard slowly got down from a donkey cart, leaned on his staff, and walked to the crowd standing around the two on the ground.

The men explained what had happened. One said, "I say they are evil. Let them lie. We have shaded them until you came. If we take the shade away, we do nothing; and the sun will take them soon."

The old man watched the men on the ground breathe and looked up at his friends, "Do not let men you do not respect set your standards . . . what would Christ do?" He turned and walked back to his cart.

Men of the crowd picked up the two and carried them to the nearest house. They propped them up in bed, cleaned their wounds, prized their mouths open and dribbled water on their tongues. After a few hours, the two unconscious men would swallow small amounts of liquids. Some of the men sat at the bedside and gave sips of water and juices from a cup almost continuously. In the heat of midday, one man waved a fan.

On the third day, David began to move and grab at the arm above him. After hours of purposeless movements, he opened his eyes. He slowly realized he was hearing strange words and struggled to answer. Amnon woke later in the day. David said to his son, "Wake up and help me remember why we are in this strange place and what we have done. I hope my memory is nothing but a nightmare. I remember the explosion. I think it blew the shadows from my mind." When they were alone, they both remembered and regretted the same events.

After they ate solid food and gained strength another day, David spoke to several of the men outside the house. "I remember you didn't want us to blow the side off that old monument of your ancestors to build the straight road. How much did we damage it?"

"Only a hole in the side, but it opens to a cave over the big spring. We have not been in it. There may be angry spirits."

The next morning, they walked to the opening and shined a flashlight into the cavity. They tied ropes to make a crude rope ladder, hooked it around one of the blocks blasted away and climbed down into darkness. In the dim light they saw water bubbling up to make a spring that flowed out of the bottom to create the spring in the sun that all the men knew. David and Amnon shivered. After coming from the sunshine above, air was cold around the water. Human skeletons were clustered at one side of the cave. Little flesh hung on the bones. On the opposite side lay a single skeleton--larger than the others. David stood closer and shined the light on the left hand. The man had died holding something thicker than David's thumb and longer than his palm. David pulled it loose from the bones. Even in death the man had held it tight. There were at least eight flat surfaces on the side. One end had a flat slightly wavy surface and was clear. The other end came to a point. The sides and pointed end were black, like they were coated with paint or pitch. Only the flat end was clear. David shined his flashlight into that end. There was a cluster of specks deep in the crystal that seemed to reflect light. It felt like ice in his hand. The bravest of the men above had come down the ladder. The three looked at the cluster of bones and the carvings on the walls. The crystal seemed to come to life in the heat of David's hand. The flat end began to glow. Dots of lights shined in a spiraling cluster on the opposite wall and slowly rotated--first slow, then faster. David felt a strange sensation and looked away. The man from above said, "Now that I am here, I hope I can get back out."

When he spoke, David turned and the circle of spinning lights struck the man in the face. His expression changed. At almost the same time, Amnon gave his usual flip answer, "Just flap your wings like a butterfly and fly out." The man began moving his arms up and down vigorously.

It took David almost a minute to understand what had happened. He remembered reading about the effect of spiraling dots. He walked closer and held the spinning lights in the man's face. "When I say 'now' you will wake and have no memory of butterflies . . . Now."

The man gave a little jerk, blinked and said, "Let's go back up. It's cold in this place."

When they climbed to the sun again, David told the waiting men. "I don't think we have done much damage to the temple of your ancestors. Move those blocks we blasted out and close the side again. The edges of some are broken, but it will look almost the same. Now you know the spring begins in this temple and is guarded forever by some of your ancestors." The crystal in David's pocket cooled and was quiet.

The next morning David said to his son, "We survived two sticks of dynamite. Now we have to ask why we were spared. Disease from this place has ruined our bodies and our lives. We must go back. We can stop this madness of an evil man. We will go on the riverboat to the city. The plane will bring supplies soon. We will fly back with then."

"Will he know we are coming? He may have spies even in this place."

"We have to hope there are none here. We can tell the pilots to be silent. I don't know what this crystal is or where it came from, but it was given to us for a reason. You saw what it did. We will use it again. The ancient ones we found in the temple lost their lives because of it. The man holding it must have been lured in and walled up in darkness. Others must have seen the danger in its power to control a person's mind and will."

They rode a donkey cart to the river, then the boat to the city with the airfield. The plane made several stops, but eventually reached the city they knew so well. With help from the crystal, they convinced the pilot and copilot to be silent about their passengers.

David said, "We cannot rest. We must rent a car and act quickly before we are seen by people we cannot control. He has spies everywhere in this city."

They were not expected and had problems at the steel door. David looked into the camera and was convincing with the story of an urgent matter that caused an emergency trip without notification. As they entered the waiting room, David pulled out the crystal from his coat pocket. The man at the desk looked up into a cluster of spinning dots of light. They checked his appointment book. "There is an appointment for two men at three." They watched while the man called and rescheduled the visit.

While the clerk was dazed by the light, Amnon thumbed through a book of phone numbers on the desk and made a call. When he heard an answer, he said, "I am sorry." He hung up on the shouted words, "Who is this?" They instructed the clerk and left. David parked their car near a shoe store.

Amnon said, "New shoes for this afternoon?"

"I can't go in with my hand in my pocket; he is watchful for even a suggestion of weapons. I will get a pair of shoes too wide and long. I can cut an opening for that crystal and push it in. As I sit down, I slide it out. I will keep my hand inside my shirt next to my chest to keep it warm until we go in. If my foot doesn't warm the crystal enough, my hand will. Wing-tips will hide it best."

The man at the desk still saw them as the scheduled appointment and announced them. As they sat in the chairs, David slid out the crystal and held the flat end toward his leg. When the glow appeared, he lifted it. The face appeared at the end of the room covered by spiraling dots of lights. He didn't respond as the others had. He shouted, "Why are you here? Take that light out of my face." His words slowed, became softer and his face relaxed.

After minutes of silence, David said, "You want to go with us. You want to take a trip with us."

David and Amnon could hardly breathe in the stillness. The face in the glow said, "Go . . . with . . . you." Each word seemed to be forced out and painful.

David said, "You want to come down and walk out the door with us." Silence again, then the slow repeated words. He pushed open a panel, stepped down from the platform, came closer and the lights spun faster. "You want to ride in the car with us."

As they walked past the desk, the man in the chair jumped up. David said, "We are making an emergency trip. All appointments are canceled."

"When will you be back? I'm covered with calls now."

"Rest assured, in time to come you will know where we go and what we do."

They put their passenger in the back seat of their car, told him to sleep and drove south. After hours on the road, they stopped at a dock. It took some time to locate the captain they wanted. He violently protested, "There's a storm blowing in. I can't ask the man who works for me to risk it and I don't want to risk my own life or the boat. It's small and can't take big waves. All the other charter boats are in."

"This man owns the boat. He wants to go." Eventually, they had to show him the crystal lights.

Others condemned them as they left. They watched operation of the boat. Once started, one man could handle it. David said, "Please slow to almost stop. Do you have an emergency raft?" The captain nodded.

"Throw it over the side and put on a life preserver."

They were forced to use the light again. "Now listen carefully; you will climb down and get on that raft. When the boat moves away, you will paddle toward the shore. You will remember nothing of this trip after you started the engine."

When the captain was on the raft and moving toward shore, they slowly increased the engine speed and the boat pulled away. After several minutes, they saw another boat coming out to meet the captain.

The winds became stronger and the waves higher. David increased the speed even more, turned into the storm, secured the wheel, and walked forward on the deck. They led their prisoner to the prow of the boat, David shined the light in his face, "You are sorry for all he evil things you have done. Now, say it!" He slowly forced out the words as if each sound brought pain. "You repent of your sins and ask God's forgiveness." His words broke apart and came like a slow motion echo. David said, "You will feel those words you have said and the thoughts they bring deep within your heart and soul. They will become real to you." The man at the prow began to twitch, then jerk and writhe. His face tightened and twisted like one in agony. Amnnon and David caught him to keep him from falling overboard. They stood him up and put his hands on the rails and faced him straight ahead. David stood by him and said, "Now look at me and listen; God may come in a gentle breeze, but he may also come in an angry storm and take what He will." His face was more relaxed as David turned him to face the churning clouds. "Look straight ahead, but listen to me. In the past you lived to control other lives and the world around you. There are powers greater than yours. Now look into this storm; know it's coming and you cannot change it."

Amnon said, "Do you think that did any good?"

"I don't know about him; it made me feel better. He would never have said the words without the light. I don't know what forced repentance does for a man . . . or if it does anything. I'm glad it's not my job to judge."

Winds grew stronger and waves higher. They saw one coming that devoured the others. David held the crystal with his left hand; the spiral dots of lights whorled on the man holding the rails, but he looked into the storm and did not turn. David put his right arm around his son. The towering wave roared over the boat; when it slowly righted itself and water drained away, the rails were twisted and decks empty. A swirling light slowly twisted, turned, became smaller and disappeared in the depths of the angry sea.

* * * * * * * * * *

Headlines the next day said, "Local businessman-industrialist and associates lost at sea; boat found adrift." For the next ten days, more newspaper articles described the problems he left. A commission established to straighten his affairs found he had influenced others through drugs or other means to take over their businesses or real estate. He then used assets from one company to buy another. In theory, he owned hundreds of houses and industries in Alabama and South America. Two months later, the commission determined when obligations were met and bills paid, there was nothing left but debts for heirs, if he had any. The industrial-real estate complex was a hollow shell and existed as long as Dr. Crunchner was alive to hold it together.

* * *

Sequel

When Job parked the car at Lisa's house, he said, "You have been quiet tonight. I know you lost your job.

Do you need to tell me something else : . . something worse?"

"Over two months ago, I did a bad thing. I'll have to tell you sooner or later. You know I worked in the office that handled legal documents for my guardian. The Commission let me work until last Monday when the investigation was over. I helped them with the records. A week before he died, I typed documents to transfer this little house . . . and the car to me. I knew my guardian signed hundreds of papers and thought he might not read every one. He did sign them. The man in the waiting room signed as witness and notarized them. That's not very legal . . . and not very honest is it?"

"It may not be, but it's just. He took your father's business and your inheritance. I wish you could have typed a document for a job."

"In a way, he gave me a new job."

"How?"

"With my experience in legal documents, I got a job in a lawyer's office . . . the one who handled my annulment case . . . and for more salary. I begin next week."

"Great! That is news. So do we still wait for the big event until I make Chief Resident level? It's less than a year away."

"Tonight, if you have the license."

"No, you will have a church wedding, even if it's just us, the preacher and a witness."

"I hope I don't have to remind you; we never tell anybody how we met. If we should ever have a child, you'll have to make up a story of 'how I met your mother.' Surely that wouldn't be more than a little white lie."

Curious Wedding

Her guardian had moved her so many times, Lisa had no close friends to help, so she planned alone. She picked a church near her house. They now had their Sunday dates there and felt more comfortable in the small congregation. They sent blanket invitations to neighborhoods where she had lived. Job posted invitations on bulletin boards of units of the hospital, the OR and ER. He sent an invitation to his parents, but didn't call or visit them.

Job was at the church early; he couldn't see out, but heard an unusual number of cars coming. The music began and he cracked the side door and peeked out. Every seat was filled and a few stood at the back. At the arranged time, he walked in toward his place in the center and stopped halfway. He had two best men. One was his father. When he saw Job, he mouthed the words, "I am sorry." His mother was on the far side.

The music changed and became louder. Lisa came down the aisle--alone. Her gown was white. Two dark spots near the hem were not noticeable. When the minister said, "Who gives this woman?"

Lisa said. "My father would if he could. I give myself." There were gasps and murmurs in the congregation. At the end of the usual words of the ceremony, Lisa and Job faced each other, smiled, and held hands. They said the words together, "I take you as my friend and love for eternity . . . in life on this earth, my devotion can only increase . . . and in the time to come, if there is no love between man and woman, my memory will sustain me." Tears rolled down Lisa's cheeks. Job's eyes felt full. He turned and only Lisa saw the single tear fall on his sleeve.

They faced the pastor and were pronounced man and wife. Job turned to kiss his new wife. Lisa whispered, "Nothing serious, now."

As they walked the aisle Job said, "We didn't think anybody would come. We didn't plan on all this. What will we feed this crowd at the reception?" Job's mother and father catered the event in secret and there was food to take home.

There was no money or time for a honeymoon. Both had to be at work on Monday. Lisa and Job began life together in her little house. Lisa showered, left the bathroom in a heavy robe and said, "Your time."

Job showered, wrapped himself with the bath towel, brushed his teeth, rinsed his mouth, dried his face with the hand towel, took it down, remembered, smiled, and half expected to see Lisa against his arm.

She was . . . and her wraparound garment was a thinner shadow than before—hardly a vapor. Between breaths she said, "We've waited so long, I didn't want to slow us down any. I hope you don't mind." There was nothing under the shadow, but Lisa. Job smiled, gave her a serious kiss, put his right hand around the shadow, held his towel with the other, and they walked down the hall.

They had had a strange beginning, but that lay faded in the past. They knew where they were, where they had been, what they had done and were still in the glow and joy of this day. Lisa and Job didn't know what lay ahead, but would face it together.

Part Two

Curious Cruise

The Storm

The ship began to sway side to side; even holding the rails, they had trouble walking the narrow passageway from the dining room. They stopped several times, gripped the rail, leaned against the wall and waited until they could stand and take a few quick steps. At the end of the corridor, he put his shoulder against the wall, unlocked the door to their room and it swung with a bang when the ship tilted as if climbing a mountain. He kicked aside a sliding suitcase in the middle of the floor, dropped his stick, and they staggered to their beds. The door slammed shut as the ship topped the wave. When the ship tilted again, a brush and a lotion bottle fell from the cabinet in the bathroom, slid through the open door across the floor and clattered against the wall while they watched from bolted-in-place beds. Lights flickered, then the room was black but for a glow at the porthole. The emergencies came on a few seconds, and then full lighting came back.

She said, "I'm glad I didn't eat much at supper. It was a little rough then, but nothing like this. I may lose what little I ate."

They strained to hear the loudspeaker over screams of the wind and crashing of waves. The static filled voice said, "This is the Captain speaking. We are in a storm worse than radar indicated or we anticipated . . . much worse. We will be traveling in a direction you didn't expect. We are a small cruise ship. We must go into the waves, so they don't capsize us. Even if we had known about the storm, we could not have reached a port for refuge . . . but fortunately, in this part of the Pacific there are no land bodies for us to be thrown into. Stay in your cabins and try to get a little rest in a bed or chair. If you try to walk around, you could be thrown to the floor and injured. We are doing everything in our power to take us through."

They lay in their beds, stared at the ceiling, and tried to ignore sounds of the storm or water washing over the porthole and the few drops trickling down the wall after each wave. The next hours were much the same: a tortured ship on a convulsing sea. The ship climbed one giant wave, fell into a valley with mountains of water all around, and then climbed the next wave. Some tilted the ship so badly they had to hold to the frame to stay in the bed. They tried not to look through the porthole when lightning showed water as a mountain above their room.

At early daylight, something heavy fell toward the front of the ship. Glass broke somewhere and water sloshed in the hall, trickled under the cabin door and across the carpeted floor. There was a scraping sound the full length of the ship; the vessel shuddered, slowed, and the engines stopped. After a few seconds, they began again and the room shook as they raced then slowed to a rough idle. The room went black. Emergency lights flickered on. Minutes later, the loudspeaker came on and they strained to hear over the static. "This is the Captain; we have struck something in the water . . . probably debris from the storm. Our propellers are damaged. We can no longer turn into the waves. The next big one from the side will capsize us. We are already taking on water faster than we can pump out. The engine room is filling. We will sink. We have no choice. We must abandon ship. Distress signals have gone out. Go to the lifeboat station. The seas are rough, but lifeboats are our only chance. Crewmembers will be in both boats." Then, wind noises drowned his words. The voice came back and said, "I repeat, senior persons are not to come." The speaker clicked off and storm sounds seemed louder.

She said, "Does that mean we are expendable?"

"Sounds like it. We are probably the most senior on this ship."

There was a knock at the door. He leaned on his stick, struggled up, took two steps, braced himself against the wall and opened the door. A crewman stood with water pouring over his shoes. "You heard what he said about seniors? The Captain doesn't think older people would be able to get into a lifeboat in this wind. We'll try to get the tender over the side after the lifeboats are away. You will have something to hold to, climbing down a rope ladder. It's a bigger boat with a diesel engine and sheltered area. Give us time to get the lifeboats in the water. Come after ten minutes." He turned and ran with splashing steps.

They left after five minutes. Even with his stick and holding to the rail, he had trouble walking the tilting wet corridor. She used both hands and pulled herself along the other rail. They reached the station and watched through the glass panel in the upper half of the door, as the tender was swung over the side and lowered. Both lifeboats were climbing in the distance. Suddenly the sea seemed to fall away and the ship tilted. They saw the towering wave coming. He put his arm around her, held to the rail with both hands and pushed her against the wall. There were shouts and screams from the deck. The wave rumbled and roared, crashed against the ship and washed over the deck. The ship shook, tilted far to the other side and there was a bursting-tearing sound toward the front. When the water cleared and the ship slowly became more upright, through the cracked glass on the door they saw an empty deck. Captain, crewmembers and waiting seniors were gone. The tender scraped against the ship and then stopped. There was no engine noise. They heard nothing but sounds of the storm and bump . . . bump . . . bump of the tender on the side of the ship. They watched the same big wave break one boat in half and turn over the other. They saw open mouths, but the wind took the screams.

She said, "Those poor people. What do we do now?"

"From the sound and the way the ship shook, the pilothouse is probably gone. The Captain said the engine room was filling. I think the whole crew is gone. We saw the other passengers go. We must be the only two left. This ship is stronger than a lifeboat. It's still floating. We have no choice. We stay here. I have my flashlight in case the emergency lights go off. If I can find my stick, we go back to the room. It seems to be a little more stable than here. We took this trip for answers. After fifty years of practice, I didn't I know if I could survive without work and I didn't know if you could put up with me at home all the time. I never expected anything like this. If this is an answer, I don't know what it is."

She said, "I know one answer, but we didn't listen. When we saw how small the ship was, we should have gone back home. I don't mind eating with the crew, but the one dining room tells us how small the boat is."

Waves took the ship for hours--in some direction. He looked at his wife in the faint light and said, "I know you always wanted me to forget how we met. I have tried; I want you to know no matter what happens, I have always . . .." His words were cut off by a sudden grinding crash and shaking of the ship. Both were thrown to the floor. Sounds of things falling came from every direction. The ship twisted to one side, then straightened with a screeching grating sound and stopped with a jerk. Sounds of wind, rain and waves were still there, but the room did not move with the storm. Water ran across their arms and face to the other side of the room. He struggled to push up and pulled against the bed to a sitting position. He turned her over, dragged her to the bed, but couldn't lift her. He put a pillow under her head and lightly moved his fingers over the red area on her forehead. There was no depression. She breathed, but didn't move. When he spoke, she answered, but seemed confused. He pulled up lids and shined his flashlight in her eyes. Pupils reacted to light. After several minutes, she was able to get into bed with help. After she rested, he said, "The storm isn't throwing us around any more. We can't see much from our little porthole. You stay here, I'll go to the station where we were and try to see what happened."

She answered slowly, almost in a whisper. "No, don't leave me. I don't want you to be out of my sight."

He leaned on his stick, pulled along on the rail with one hand and she staggered along holding to his arm. Water poured down the passageway and streamed over their shoes. The floor was not quite level, but it didn't move and walking was easier than before.

New Home

Through the cracked window at the station they saw winds were much less. Across smoother water, a dark mass did not move in the storm and looked to be land. The tall center came to a peak. There was a glow at the top and steam or vapor swirled away in the wind. He said, "Look, that must be a volcano way up there. Seems to be trees on that lower slope and toward the bottom some are in a straight line. Nature doesn't do that."

"If that's an island why aren't there any beaches?"

"Beaches may not be like ones we know. Could be gray or black sand. I thought I just saw a flicker of light on that tall rise out of the trees to the right."

There was a jumble of forgotten equipment to one side of the door, either for the tender or lifeboats. He picked up a rope, tied one end around his waist and the other to the door pull, leaned against the wind, held to the rope and moved half step at the time to the twisted railing at the edge of the ship. He glanced over the side and pulled himself back. When he caught his breath he said, "There's a small boat on the back of the tender. It's just a foot or two from the water. If you help me, we can get it over the side and try for the island. I can't run the tender and couldn't paddle the little boat that far, but the wind is blowing toward the island. We must be on a reef at the edge of a lagoon. We could go over in a bad blow. Maybe the storm will die down soon."

After an hour, the wind wasn't much less, but darkness was coming and they didn't want to spend a night on the creaking ship. They took a sleeping bag from the ships store, sheets and towels from a linen closet, a little extra clothing and another flashlight. They stuffed everything in the bag, rolled and tied it along with his stick, then lowered it on a rope to the tender. He went down the rope ladder first so he could help her if she slipped. They turned the boat over and pushed it into the water. He held to the ladder, leaned over and stared down.

"What's wrong?"

"Now that it's in the water, it seems so much smaller than I thought, but it's all we've got." They threw down a smaller ladder from the tender, climbed down, sat in the boat and pulled down the bag. As soon as he loosened the rope from the tender, wind pushed the boat toward the beach. She held the bag to keep it from being blown away. He used the oars only to keep the boat facing the right direction. Winds became stronger and brought more rain. There was no way to slow the boat. They struck the beach and climbed the gray sand. She fell over the side and struck her head again. He struggled out of the boat, turned her over, held up her head, brushed the sand away, and felt her forehead. There was still no depression, but the skin on the left was more discolored and beginning to swell. She answered him, but was more confused than before. Her voice was so weak, he could hardly hear over sounds of the wind.

"Can you lie here and rest while I try to find the place where I saw the light?"

"No, don't leave me."

"We are two old people trying to move about in a strange place in a rainstorm. You'll have to walk and help me." He pulled on the boat to get them upright. He pulled his stick from the bundle, leaned on it and tried to help her walk. They staggered across the smooth beach, wobbling step at the time. Beyond the sand, he dropped his stick; they leaned against each other and he dragged her toward the gray-white mass rising in the distance. He grabbed limbs of trees and bushes with one hand and pulled his wife with the other. He stopped to catch his breath in an open area and looked up. "Look at that. Now that we're here, I don't see a light, but there's a row of steps in the middle of that ridge." They were worn in the center and had a rail on the left. He dragged her another few feet and tried the rail. It was loose, but seemed secure enough to use. He looked up toward darkness at the head of the stairs. There was something white in the shadows. He blinked and strained to see. "I think that's a man . . . a man with a long beard, but he's not moving." He shouted, "Hello, up there!"

The wind and rain slowed and they heard croaking sounds then slow strained words: "Come . . . up . . . can . . . not . . . help."

He held to the rail with his left hand and pushed her a step at the time. She collapsed at the top of the stair. He crawled around and pulled her out of the rain. She mumbled, but would not answer simple questions. The bearded man leaning on a stick in the shadows said nothing.

"My wife's been hurt and is soaking wet; I have to go back and get something to dry her and then fix a place for her to rest." He sat by his wife until his breathing was slower, then crawled to the rail, pulled himself up and began the stumbling trip down. The man in the shadows made a few strange noises, but no words. At the bottom of the stairs, croaking sounds came again and the bearded man's stick rattled down the steps. He held to the rail, leaned over, picked it up and walked slowly back to the boat. He tied the boat's rope to a tree, then dragged the sleeping bag and his own stick back to the steps. He crawled the stairway pulling the bag and sticks in near total darkness. His wife's clothes were still wet and she was shivering, but he could do nothing until his breathing slowed.

The old man did not speak when he took back his stick, but when the flashlight came on, there was a gasp and strained voice, "Light . . . no . . . fire?"

"Yes, without fire. I need the light to check her. I have to take off these wet things, if you would turn your head for a bit." He peeled outer clothing. Underclothes were wet and had smears of gray sand. He dried her with a towel covered her with a folded sheet and slowly worked her into the dry sleeping bag, put her head on the pad, and zipped the side. He had undressed this body many times, but there was no excitement or joy this night--only fear. He rolled up the wet towel for a pillow, lay by his wife, and sleep of exhaustion came in seconds.

He became aware of light and a shadow moving. The old man was holding his stick with his right hand, propping against the wall with his left, standing in the morning light staring at the two on the floor. He pushed up on his elbows slowly. His back was still wet and there was pain and stiffness in every joint. He said, "My name is Jobson--Ira Jobson. I am called Job, like the man from Uz who had so many troubles. The sleeping lady is my wife. I'll introduce her when she wakes."

The old man moved his mouth and made sounds, but there were no words. Then in a low strained voice he forced the words, "I . . . am . . . Adam." After several croaking tries, he said, "Voice . . . gone. Not . . . used. He pointed to a large bin like structure and said, "Food." He picked up something from the top.

"Both . . . eat . . . one." He offered the remains of what had been a large cluster of dried brown fruits, wrinkled like dates or prunes, but smaller. He took one for himself and ate it, as if to show they weren't poison. Adam watched while Job pinched the fruit into bits and forced it in the woman's mouth. She swallowed, but would not open her eyes or respond to her husband's voice.

Job crawled across the floor and pulled up on the rail at the top of the stairs to stand and look at their refuge for the night. They were in a cave with a floor to ceiling opening for the stairs. To his left toward the sea, an oval opening was just above a table and the width of the table. The ceiling was rounded and natural, but the floor had been crudely leveled. One chair was by the table at the opening toward the sea. A bed was in the center and another chair toward the stairs. All were wood bound together with vines. Shelves on the bin Adam pointed to were almost empty. The old man leaning on a stick was little more than five feet, with wrinkled face, small eyes, and a huge swollen spreading nose with parts of the rim hanging like icicles into his beard. The hair and beard were long, dingy white, and disheveled. His mustache was not trimmed, but parted to show some of his lips. He blew loose hair away and pulled his chin down before he tried to speak. Arms and what showed of legs were thin. His large feet were bare with long nails. He moved his toes like a purring cat as if feeling the roughness of the floor, He wore a single garment: a coarsely woven pale brown gown with slits for his head and arms with a dull green strap tied around his waist.

At the back of the cave, a stream of water came through a hole above, flowed in a channel almost waist high, and poured through an opening toward the sea. By signs and grunted words Adam made Job understand that he drank from the left, washed in the middle, and the right was for bodily functions. Job ate one of the strips of dried fruit and drank water from a clay cup. The fruit was almost like leather; the water was tepid and smelled faintly of sulfur.

The old man pointed to the square planting of trees beyond the steps. With slow painful words, he asked if Job could pick fresh fruit and handed him a worn basket of woven vines and a small wedge-shaped black stone with a sharp edge.

Job leaned on his stick and walked slowly to the grove. The natural growth up the slope to the sides had trees 50 feet tall or more and were unlike any he had ever seen. There were clusters of strange leaves at the top and few branches on the trunk. The canopy was so thick, little sunlight reached the forest floor. A few trees to the far right were shorter, thicker, and had leaves like ferns. Remains of large trees lay in the square grove. They had been girdled, then died and fell--toward the south. When the leaves were gone and sky was clear, Adam had planted rows of small trees. He had cut tops as they grew to make lower branches so he could reach the fruit on younger trees. Bird voices stopped when Job walked into the grove, but began again unless he moved or made noise. Seabirds were under the trees eating fruit knocked off by birds above. Some of the birds in the trees were huge and unfamiliar. Some looked like eagles or hawks, but were eating fruit beside the others. He heard something moving in the dry leaves by his feet. He jumped back in fear of a snake, but it was a huge millipede. A bird saw it at the same time, picked it up and flew away. Job picked one orange, one yellow fruit--

each oval and a little larger than a grapefruit--and a cluster of small pink fruits. He didn't try to reach the lemon sized green ones farther up the slope. He stopped to rest and watched two dragonflies circling a pond in a stream coming down the slope. The blue wings over a foot across glowed in the sunlight.

Even the two single fruits and the cluster made a heavy load pulling on the rail up the steps. Adam cut the fruits with a sharp stone wedged in a wood block, raised one of the slices to his nose, nodded, and pointed to Job. Fresh fruit was moist and good--nothing like the dry strip with no flavor. Adam showed how to pour the water back and forth to lose the sulfur smell. Job reached for the pink fruit. Adam shook his head, moved very slowly leaning on his stick, picked up the cluster, and put them in the sun at the top of the stairs. Job lifted his wife's head and she was able to swallow a little water. He checked her eyes and forehead.

A bird left the grove and flew to the top of the rail, ignored Adam and flew into the cave and landed on the table then to the floor. The bird was larger than a crow, with a thick bill and iridescent black feathers that seemed to glow even in the shadows. The bird walked the edges of the cave, behind the food bin and the table legs. It found one long thin beetle and another thicker with pinchers. When it left, Adam waved, turned to Job and said, "My . . . helper."

Job moved one of the rickety chairs, sat by his wife, and stared down. She still wouldn't answer, but when he pinched the side of her neck, she frowned, opened her eyes, looked around, gasped and said, "What is this place?" Before Job could answer, there was sudden motion in the sleeping bag and she said, "I have nothing on. Where are my clothes?"

Job said, "They were wet and filled with sand. I took then off."

"I was undressed by a total stranger while I was asleep?"

"What do you mean stranger? Look at me. Don't you know me?"

"I've never seen you before in my life."

"Then what is your name?"

"It's . . . uh . . . I don't know." She began crying and pulled away when Job tried to comfort her.

"What's the last thing you do remember?"

"A storm. A terrible storm . . . and I fell and hit my head . . . in the sand . . . dirty sand."

"Where is your home?"

"Uh . . . I . . . I don't know."

He handed her a small bundle. "Here are some dry things. See if you can manage to dress in the bag. We'll turn our head anyway."

They heard rustling sounds and then another gasp. "I have on a wedding ring. I'm married. I have a home; I have a husband; I belong to somebody . . . but I don't know who."

She sobbed again—this time louder. Adam leaned against the table, pointed with his stick. "You . . . said . . . wife."

"Don't say that when she stops crying and can hear you. She has amnesia-- maybe related to the head injury. She has no memory from before the storm. It may come back later today, tomorrow . . . or never. I can't force her to accept me; anything startling could destroy her."

After she dressed, got out of the bag and ate some of the strange fruit, Job said, "The sky is clear and looks like the tide is going down. I have thought of a way to get back to the ship. I sure can't paddle against that wind.

"His wife said, "No, don't leave me!"

"You said I was a total stranger."

"You are . . . the words just came out; I don't know why."

"Watch from the top of the stairs. I will be in sight most of the time."

The lagoon was bounded on the west by steep black cliffs rising from the water's edge, but on the east and south by a gray, almost-black beach. Trees covered the slope to the south. The north end of the lagoon had a coral reef that was the source of spray and fog at low tide. The storm had washed the ship through a natural pass or when it struck it tore an opening in the reef and was grounded toward the east beach. The water was just deep enough to reach the ship with the small boat at low tide. Job put his stick in the gray sand and pulled himself, the rope, and boat along the edge of the calm water. He stopped to rest several times and fell once. Job struggled to push up from the sand with his stick, but couldn't. He pulled on the rope, crawled into water and pulled up on the boat. Eventually, by walking the beach he was well beyond the ship. At low tide there was less water between the sand and ship. He got in the boat, pushed away from the beach with his stick and drifted in the breeze to the tender. With the lower water, he had trouble climbing the rope ladder at the back, then up the other ladder onto the ship. He sat and rested several minutes then loaded as much as he dared put in the small boat. As soon as he untied the rope, the wind from the north pushed him back toward the beach near the cave. His wife was standing at the head of the stair when he brought the first load. The day and Job's strength were gone when he struggled up the last time.

The next morning, Job sat by his wife and recited a list of names to see if she could recognize her own. He tried to say hers no different than the others. He couldn't, but she didn't notice. She said, "I don't know any of those people."

"I guess we still have to call you 'the woman' until you remember your name or pick a new one. "Job stared at his wife in her confusion. *The face I knew and loved so is hers, but the looks she gives me and her words are not. Even her walk is different. Her steps are unsure. I can't stop myself from thinking it, but that's the last time I'll say her name aloud until she comes back . . . if she does come back. All I can do is try to protect her from dangers she can't remember . . . while I hope and wait.*

Over the days that followed, Job brought plates, knives, cups and things Adam had forgotten or never seen. They ate as much as they wanted of the yellow, green, and orange fruits, but only one wrinkled brown fruit each day. Days stretched into weeks. Many mornings there was light rain, but there was always steam swirling down from the volcano, geysers toward the top, and fog drifting from the lagoon. Some days the volcano rumbled, shook the cave, spewed fire, and poured out a short lava stream. The first time Job and his wife were startled, Adam said, "Voice . . . like . . . thunder . . . tell . . . of . . . sins."

At quieter times, Job explored the lower tree-covered slopes. Adam told him where to cut a type of brush limb he burned continuously like a candle. He warned of huge scorpions hiding between rocks and the pretty red fruit on a low bush. Birds knew better, but it had caused death in a few rats that tried it.

In one of his circular trips to the ship, Job found the manual for the tender. He started the diesel motor and ran it enough to charge the battery. There was a radio on the boat, but it was dead. The one on the ship had been torn away by the big wave. Even portable radios and cell-phones in the cabins were soaked and ruined. On another day, he built up his courage, dropped the tender the last few feet to the water at high tide and made a run for the beach. The bottom leaked so badly, they would have lasted little longer than lifeboats in the storm. He brought tools, nails and screws in the little boat and they built a third chair and a screen for the "bodily functions" part of the stream across the cave.

He brought two cots and bedding from the ship. He first put them far apart, but his wife wanted him nearby. She still saw him as a stranger, but for reasons she couldn't explain, wanted him near.

Job brought combs, makeup, and creams for his wife; most were her own, but she didn't know it. One day, in a cabin at the far end of the ship he finally found a handheld mirror not broken in the crash. When he got back to the cave, he handed it to his wife. She took it, sat in the bright light at the table by the opening toward the sea, stared into the glass, touched her cheeks, her lips, her hair, and said, "I know you; you are me . . . but what is your name?" She finished combing her hair and left the mirror on the table propped against the wall.

When she left, Adam sat in the same chair, stared in the glass, and began sobbing. Job put a hand on his shoulder. "What's wrong?"

Adam touched his nose. He struggled, made sounds, and words finally came, "Look . . . not . . . meet . . . maker . . . like . . . this. Some . . . potion . . . will . . . help?"

Job said, "You know He doesn't see you as you are-- either body or soul. You have rhinophyma . . . about as bad as I've seen. The skin on your nose is thick and deformed. Medicines won't help. You know I'm a surgeon. At low tide tomorrow, I'll look on the ship to see if I can find what I need--that is, if you want to risk surgery in this remote place. Things have to go perfectly; we can't handle a complication. You'll be slow to heal and the skin will be thin."

Adam nodded and said, "Small . . . nose?"

"Yes, I carve it like a bar of soap or piece of soft wood; I can do it only if I can find the tools and medicines to keep you from feeling pain."

"Even . . . no medicine."

Job found everything but blades in the Ship Surgeon's office. He found a surprise instrument. Job hadn't seen a battery heat cautery in years. This one was old, but he hoped it still worked. He spent almost an hour in the ship's store working by flashlight and had about given up when he found the blades. They had been pulled from the shelf long ago and put in a dusty box with other things no longer called for.

Adam was sitting at the head of the stairs as Job carried up his supplies.

"Now?"

"Not today. You don't want a tired surgeon for something like this. I'll set up and do it in the morning. Scrub your nose and face with this soap now and at bedtime. I need good light of midmorning." He didn't say that he wanted time to build up courage to use ancient instruments for a bloody operation on a remote island.

Island Surgery

They moved Adam's bed to the light at the head of the stairs. Adam lay down and Job propped his head up with one chair and sat in another at the bedside. Job put ointment in Adam's eyes, scrubbed his face, injected local anesthesia to block the nose and put drapes around the nose and mouth. He injected IV sedation, put on gloves and began. He picked up one of the blades from the soak solution. He squeezed the tip of the nose with his left hand, held the double-edge razor blade crossways between his right thumb and index, bent the blade to fit the surface, moved it back and forth, and carved the nose. He did the sides and midline, then released the tip, carved it and the rim around the openings. His wife helped until blood flowed. Topical thrombin packs controlled much of the bleeding. The battery-operated hot cautery did work on large vessels. As the wire loop glowed, sizzled, and burned, it closed the bleeders. The battery died before he finished. He clamped the last bleeders with a hemostat and then held pressure. When the nose was shaped, smoothed, and bleeding controlled, Job put on non-adherent dressing. Adam began to mumble as Job took off the drapes and cleaned the face and beard. He parted the beard at the chin, used a hemostat to jerk out two long hairs and stuck them on a strip of tape. Adam frowned, opened his eyes a few seconds and tried to touch his face. Job held his arms and stayed with him until he was fully awake. Adam struggled to sit up and Job pushed him down. "Lie on your back with your head elevated. We'll begin compresses soon. When you're more awake, you can have something to eat."

"Is . . . done?"

"Your nose is shaped like a 20 year old, but it's like raw meat."

With almost constant compresses over the next few days, the surface grew a new layer of epithelium from the deep glands that were left. Job was anxious until it began to close. If he had cut below the glands, healing would take months and distort the nose with a terrible scar.

Days later, the two sat in good light at the table. Job took off the dressing and held the mirror for Adam. He turned one way then the other and stared. The smile showed, even through the beard. Job said, "It's healed; the skin is very thin, but will thicken some with time. Keep the sun off of it. When you've finished admiring yourself, I want some straight answers and don't even try to tell me you can't talk. When you had sedation, you spoke as easily as I do. Your problem is spasm, tightness, and straining your voice box. Relax, don't strain, speak softly and tell me a few things. You are different than you were when we came. I saw you walk the steps without a stick a week ago. I am different; I'm old too, but now I see better, hear better and walk anywhere without my stick. Look at these two hairs I pulled out of that long beard while you were out from the medicine. The long thin part is white; toward the middle it's gray with dark streaks, then white again and the part at the root is brown. I couldn't find hair dye for my wife, but when I saw her in good light, I knew she didn't need it. I want to know what goes on . . . and now. Remember, I know you can talk."

Adam stared at the sea for several minutes and began with a hesitant voice, little more than a whisper. Words came after several tries. "I will try to shape my words like yours. Your speech is different than I remember. I was not a young man when I was washed up on this island . . . like you. I never wanted for food. I ate my yellow or orange manna. Even tall trees drop fruit when it is overripe and birds peck it. I found this cave and shaped it a little . . . with tools of hard rock I found toward the volcano. I began to get weaker and knew the end was near . . . so I gathered a supply of dried fruit, sat at the table, watched the tides, and waited to die. I had cut a cluster of the little pink fruit . . . , tasted it . . . didn't like it, and threw it down by the head of the stair. After days in the sun, the fruits dried, wrinkled and turned brown. I watched a rat eat one of the fruits. I didn't have the energy to kill him or run him away; I had pity on him because he was old and could hardly move. I waited and watched the sea; when I heard noises, I looked at the rat. He ate and left each day. Days passed—how long, I don't know. One morning, I realized the rat scampered about like he had just been weaned. I knew it was the same rat because he had lost most of his tail in some past conflict. I didn't believe in magic, but I did eat what the rat left. Can you believe . . . eating what a rat left? The dry fruit has a different taste from the fresh. The big cluster lasted a long time. After many days, I was strong enough to gather another to dry." Adam looked at Job. "I didn't think you would believe in magic either."

Job glanced at the sea and then to Adam. "We read of miracles and may even see one. I think your survival and ours on this strange island was miraculous, but there is no magic in our world. Some may call things magic if they don't understand what they see. Nobody knows what makes us grow old. Our body constantly repairs itself and makes new cells."

"What are cells?"

"The smallest unit of our body organs. If your body were a building, they would be the tiny bricks . . . too small to see without magnification. There are different cells bound together to make our parts. These cells don't last a lifetime. It's normal for some to die. Another cell divides and a new cell is made to replace the old one. After we're grown, when a cell is replaced it's not the same. Nobody understands how the message comes and says, 'make a new cell, but make it older.' There must be an enzyme, hormone or chemical in that brown fruit that changes that message. After all, some animals like snakes don't appear to age."

Adam said, "I'm not through. I enjoyed a second youth for a time, then melancholy possessed me and I determined to let age come. I only took the fruit again to live long enough to help you. Now you have to decide what you will do."

Job stared at Adam and said, "Right now, I think I will get us some fresh fruit for lunch."

When he got back Adam was sitting at he bottom of the stair with his hat pulled down over his face. Job put the fruit on the bin.

* * *

New Name and New Adam

Job's wife was sitting at the table staring out to sea. The light glowed through her hair and outlined the body he knew so well. He was overwhelmed by the memory of love he was denied. He sat in the other chair and looked at her. "I know it's hard to be in a strange land and have no past." He reached over and put his hand on hers.

She said, "I have flashes of faces in my mind. Some are children, but I can't remember who they are. Sometimes, I close my eyes and see a house and streets, then my headache comes back; I open my eyes and see nothing, but this . . . this place." She jerked away. "I don't want any man to touch me. I belong to somebody, but I can't remember who." She pushed the ring on her finger closer to her hand.

Job stood and stared down at her. "Then you have chosen your name."

"What name?"

"We can't keep calling you 'the woman.' You can't pick one. We have to give you a name. In the life we left, one person might say to another, 'You know Sara?' The other might say 'Sara who?' So your last name will be 'Who.' First name could be Ima."

"Ima Who . . . that doesn't sound like a real name . . . unless I'm oriental. I don't know a single Chinese word; I don't think I'm oriental."

"It may not sound like a name, but it will be yours until you remember your real one."

One day was much like another: eat fruit, sweep the cave, watch the sea, listen to the birds, walk on the beach or up the slope and an occasional trip to the ship. Food was a few steps away; life seemed secure and peaceful . . . then the volcano rumbled and reminded them there is always danger--somewhere. Adam complained that since his shipwreck he had done nothing other than care for himself, until Job and Ima came. He said he had no other purpose in life, now that he had helped the two survive.

As they sat around the table, Adam frowned and stared at the sea. Job said, "I bought some things from the ship today to cheer you up. Your nose looks young; it doesn't match your hair and whiskers. You need a haircut." He brought out scissors and clippers. "Sit still and I'll do head and face."

While Adam protested, Job grabbed the beard, made a swipe with the scissors and amputated almost half of it. Job held it up and said, "Now, lets even it up a little. "He grabbed the hand-operated clippers and shaped the beard, leaving less than an inch of brown hair. "That face looks good--now for the part where you live." Adam jerked away, but the clippers pulled to stop him, "Let me cut it to match your face. Be still or I might cut an ear. I haven't seen 'em, but you must have two somewhere under all that brush." He left the hair longer than the beard, giving a gray layer over brown. He held up the mirror. "Look at Adam of the past. Now you'll have to wash your ears."

He twisted his head back and forth and said, "I was never like this."

Job said. "I found something to exercise your brain inside that fresh clipped head." He took a stack of papers from a box and put them on the table. "Here is something you have never had on this island that seems to furnish everything: ink and paper to write on and a practice pad, in case you have lost some of your letters,"

"I have no pen staff or quill."

"I'll show you how to fill this fountain pen. Now write your life story or what you remember of the land you left behind. One more thing: I brought books . . . including a Bible."

"I don't remember. I cannot read it."

"It'll come back." Job turned a few pages. "Look, right here it says, *In the beginning* . . . . That's always a good place to start."

Job left him staring at the book and moving his lips as his finger slowly traced the words.

The Boat

Job ran along the beach, but stopped when he saw Ima stumble in the wet sand at the water's edge; he reached out his hand. She pulled away.

"Why are you running?"

"Because I can. It's been a long time. For the first time in years, I feel free. I can leave the stick behind."

"That was a nice thing you did for Adam."

"We owe him our lives. We might not have survived without his help,"

Ina nodded and said, "Where are you . . . are we going now?"

"I want to look at the bottom of the boat."

At low tide, the tender rested on the sand and leaned to the left, so Job could go over one entire side. There were no obvious holes, but the wood had shrunk and the cracks had not been caulked or painted in years.

"What will you do?"

"Try to fill the cracks. I'll look for something on the ship."

As they sat at the table in the late afternoon, Job told Adam of his problem with the tender. "To make our lives more comfortable, I would like to haul more than I can move in that little boat."

Adam looked through the opening to the sea and then toward evening shadows beyond the steps and said, "I've told you this island has furnished everything I need--not what I wished for--but what I needed to live. I have had problems finding it at times. There is a tree that yields a pitch like none you have ever seen. It's far up the slope, but I think I can make the trip. I will show you tomorrow. We have to wait for light of midmorning."

After a light rain the next morning, Job looked at the bright sunshine for almost an hour and said, "Things should be dry now. Is it time to go?"

Adam said, "You are not ready." He wrapped Job's ankles and lower legs with a strip of material like he wore and tied on a sheet of tree bark. He said, "You might need this." When they began, Adam used his walking stick with his right hand and with his left carried a thicker shorter stick. The end was split and a rock tied in the opening with vines. Job asked about it. Adam said, "We might need it. I am sorry, but you have to carry the other things; I may need my sick to walk the slope."

In the shadows of the trees, Adam moved slower and slower. Job said," Is this climbing too much for you? Should we rest a while?" He saw Adam bad swapped sticks from one hand to the other.

"I am looking. Stop! Do not move." He swung the thick stick in his right hand. After the sound of the blow, there was a writhing at the base of a tree.

"What is that?"

Adam struck again and when the writhing stopped, he turned something over with his stick and dragged it out of the deep shadows. "I call it a snazard."

Job said, "That looks like a snake--a thick snake--but it's got four short legs. Does he walk on those legs?"

"He moves like a snake, but uses the legs too. You need protection from his bite. I learned the hard way, years ago. I made it back to the cave and took two of the brown fruits--for what good that would do--before I passed out. I have no idea if one day or ten had passed when I woke. A bite still hurts, but I no longer react like that first time. Days later, I went back to the same place I was bitten. That snazard became the belt I wear. You have seen the rats and all the different birds; if we move slowly, we may see the only other walking beast on this island."

Trees in the cluster Adam found high on the slope were leaning only slightly. The wind from the north seemed less at this elevation. They were twisted, had hard knots on the trunk, streaks down the side and hard clumps at the base. Moss and small ferns were evidence that clumps of resin from wounds were years old. With Adam directing him, Job made a long cut with a hatchet and hung a bucket bent to fit against the tree. The sap dripped almost in a stream. Adam said, "It is like water now. Let this dry in the sun a little and it will make a stiff pitch to seal the cracks. Use it as paint before it thickens. It hardens like iron. I used it on the steps many years ago and I painted this stick. It is the blood of the tree, so it will be pale red when dry. I can beat a tree limb to make a brush, if you don't find one on the ship."

They sat and waited until the bucket filled. On the way down Adam said, "Stop now!" and pointed. A cat-like creature was moving away with two little ones. It was dark, dappled-gray and almost impossible to see when still in dense shade. When it turned, the face was more like a bear. Adam said, "I think the ancestor of the shadow-cat may have come after a very early shipwreck. It's now certainly larger than any housecat I remember. I have no idea where the green snazard came from. You have seen the birds, now you have seen the walking beasts. The rat is on the low end. It gets eaten by the others. The snazard will kill and eat the cats and rats . . . and birds. The head is bigger than a snake. It has more teeth than just fangs and can bite out chunks. I have tried to run most of the cats and snazards up the slope, but when the cat is hungry enough, it sneaks to the gray beach that matches the color of the thin coat and lies at the water's edge. If a fish comes close, it becomes dinner. I have told you I have no desire for meat; now you know why. I will not eat birds. When I thought I was about to

die, they called me to the fruit. I could eat fish, but my
years on the sea turned me against anything in the
water."

* * *

The sap thickened in the sun. The next day, Job
cleaned the cracks, used a putty knife to push in the
pitch, wiped the surface with a rag and smoothed it with
a stone. The next day, he made a slow careful trip up the
slope for more of the strange tree sap and painted the
caulked side. Tilting the boat and working on the other
side took another two days. After it dried, he propped
the boat level with wedges. Fumes were more than he
could stand in a closed space. He used a mask and
oxygen tank from the ship and gave a quick coat to the
inside. He dug out sand around the boat so the back half
floated at high tide.

Decision Time

Late in the day, Job walked the steps and sat at the
table. "Adam, I want to talk. We owe our lives to you . .
. and this strange island. I've tried to understand your
life. You had no choice; you had no way to leave. You
have become a part of this island and it is part of you; it
gave you life. It's your family. It was forced on you, but
your needs were met in this strange place. There's great
comfort here. There is no dismal winter. Every bird sings
when the sun shines. This island is not my family."

Adam said, "When I came, all those things I have
were strange to me and not easy to come by."

"Yes, but they were there for you to find and not far
away. Here there is no gloom of winter. There is no
challenge. For me—I see challenge all around: the sea. It
separates me from the world I knew. I feel the pull of the
land and family I left behind. Most men and women are
social beings and we all need to have purpose in our life.
Yours was to save us, though you didn't know why you
were left for years. Your nose surgery was the only

operation I've done in the past year. I cannot do what I was trained to do--what I was meant to do. I am old, but I am--or was--still working. It's confusing now that I have a stronger step when I walk and see a younger face in the mirror. With the bottom of the tender sealed tight and painted, I am thinking of trying it against that wind from the north. I have made it to the ship with the tender. I think I can head into that stronger wind and get beyond the reef and out of the lagoon. I don't know where I'll go, because I don't know where we are. There is nothing but a compass left on the boat to help me. I will head east and a little to the north. If I can get in one of the shipping lanes, I may get some help." He looked from one to the other. "Will the two of you go with me?"

Ima said, "If my life is back there, I'll go. You must promise to not touch me. You know I don't know who I belong to."

They looked at Adam. "You are asking me to go to go to a land filled with strange people with their lives run by machines like the one that pushes that boat?"

"We do use machines to get from here to there. It's far quicker and easier than walking or riding an animal and we use them to perform work for us."

"You use them to think for you, too. Before it died, that little thin box

you brought did." Adam frowned and stared at the sea, as if answers lay in the waves. After several minutes he began. "When I was thrown into the sea, I thought my life was about to end. I prayed to be saved and delivered to my home and family. I washed up on that hard gray beach, a dying broken man. Why should I, a sinful man, live and good men on my ship drown. I lay on the sand without strength to move, aware of nothing. A bird pecked my finger and woke me. I heard others calling from the fruit trees. I knew there was life here. It must have taken me an hour to drag myself to those sounds of life. I found fruit on the ground. After I ate, I crawled up a ridge to the cave. From the opening, I called out time after time with what strength I had. Sounds of the birds stopped when I called and I heard nothing. Then the bird-calls came back. Nobody was on this island. After I slept, I called again and heard a rumble from the mountain. I knew no man lived here, but God was here. He hasn't given me what I yearned for and asked for. I was here and alive. He has given me what I needed. I thought there must be something more for me to do, or I would not have been spared. After years of waiting, I had given up and was almost too weak to help you. Now, I have finished my work. The world you go back to would be too strange for me to endure. Any family I ever knew is long gone. I will spend the time God allows me on this island that has given me life these many years."

"I wish you would go. I know nothing about boats."

"Before you leave, I will teach you what I know."

They said nothing for several minutes. Job said, "One more thing . . . could we have some seeds of those strange trees to take with us?"

"I thought you might want to go; I potted plants two weeks ago--the same day I quit the brown fruit. I have two of each. You will have seeds, if you take some fresh fruit. The pink fruit has a single seed that sticks to the stem when it dries. The plants are not animals, but you could still call your boat 'The Ark.'"

"Why would you quit something that keeps you alive?"

"I have done what I was put here to do. You are the first in all these years. There will be no others. My ears are better now and rumbles from above seem louder. That old mountain--with a fire in its throat--may blow one day. It has threatened for years. I do think about rivers of lava coming down the slope and pouring over me . . . sounds too much like fires of Hell. That's why I built my 'safe place.' I will help with your boat, but I will stay."

"Safe place . . . what is a safe place?"

"You know this big piece of rock has holes and tunnels in it; there was a long one under the water trough. I extended it and made a chamber beyond the trough where I can sit. The far end of that tunnel had a small opening toward the sea. The wind from the north blows through it and out the hole for the tunnel door. You may not have noticed the door. It's fitted so well, you probably thought it was a crack."

"Food and water?"

"I keep a little dried fruit there and water is simple; there is a small hole in the bottom of the water trough; when I pull the plug I get water. I can't last more than a few days, but I had rather starve than burn. I have used it when storms were bad."

"It must have taken forever to carve that place."

"What else did I have to do in the years I waited for you to come? I had to fill my days or go mad. You would never believe how long it took me to make the thread and weave this garment I wear. I cut stalks of a plant I found to the west, soaked them in the sea near coral, beat them and then spun the fibers and wove the thread on a frame of thorns. You must take all the brown fruit . . . even some fresh clusters to dry. They must last until your plants mature."

The next morning they climbed the ladder to the boat. Adam stood on the covered deck portion, pointed at the center, and said, "What are these boards covering? The ends are not even and they have never been painted."

Job prized them up to expose the end of a broken mast. "So this was once a sailboat?"

"Too small . . . probably for flags and banners. You could put up a small sail if you can find canvas."

"How can I cut a mast?"

"Bring a saw and an axe. I told you what's needed will be furnished. I hope the trees are still there; they are useless to me and I haven't seen them in years. The wood is stronger and different from any you know."

Adam had to use his stick to climb the western slope of the mountain. They watched carefully, but saw none of the animals other than two rats when they began. The grove on the far side of the mountain was different from all the others. The canopy of treetops was so thick and the shade so dense it seemed like night. Few seeds would germinate--if they did, they would wither and die. In this darkness, long shoots had come from heavy roots touching the surface of the ground and had grown toward the sky. They had no bark like their parents, but were covered with a smooth hard coat with little color. When the shoot reached the light of an opening, leaves filled out and they struggled against the others. Job measured the base and cut a straight shoot. Adam said, "I know you are thinking of strength. It will dry quickly and be strong. My rail at the steps has been there in the weather for years. Now cut two thinner pieces."

"I have the big one. Why little ones?"

" For a yard. You have to hang the sail on something."

On the beach, Job scraped the surface and propped up the future mast and yards to dry. He stood them straight and protected from the wind. He had a harder time pulling out the remains of the old mast. He took the tender to the ship, found a rectangular canvas, and filled plastic cans with diesel.

Job made it back to the cave almost at dark. "I have bad news for two of us. I have loaded cans of fuel. The boat is settling into the water so, I don't see how we can load water or anything else."

Ima said, "Sounds like your boat needs water wings."

Job laughed, thought a while, and said, "Ima, you might have said that as a joke, but you may have something there. Anything I do with boats will be weird because I know nothing about them. I've seen a big rubber raft on the ship . . . looked new. I'll see what I can work out."

The raft had a large inflatable cylinder at the edge to support people sitting in the flat center. Job took it to the beach, inflated the sides, cut away most of the center, folded the rest against the boat, tied it with ropes around the boat front to back and others to the top.

When he backed out into the lagoon, it seemed to lift the boat higher in the water.

Over the next few days, he loaded things from throughout the ship. The safe was open. He took packets of bills--all hundreds, the ship's log and anything of value in the cabins. These were worthless on the island, but would be useful in the world they were going back to. He picked up his wife's passport and billfold, looked at the picture on her driver's license a long time and put it in the box of other valuables. He divided these into piles and wrapped them in paper, made a trip to the twisted trees for another bucket of resin, painted the paper, and stuck a vine handle on each package. Adam insisted he take two collections of stones he had gathered over the years and papers he had written. Job loaded cans of water and put the small woven vine pots of plants under a tinted sheet of plastic from the ship for the days when they left the island's shield of warm fog. With the 'water wings,' the boat seemed high enough to accept food and passengers. The mast and yards did dry quickly. With Adam's help, Job put them in place and painted the deck. He cut, sewed, and hung the canvas he found in the ship then attached a rope ladder to reach the sail.

As they finished, Adam said, "A square sail doesn't use the wind best, but it's easier to make and easier to handle for a man new to sailing."

As they sat eating their fruit, Job said, "We are nearly loaded, but it may be for nothing. I know where the pass in the reef is. I think we can make it through at high tide, but I don't know if I can fight that wind from the north very long. We can't carry fuel to take us far; we have to hope and pray for a different wind in our little sail to take us north and east until we find a ship."

The volcano rumbled louder than usual and shook the cave. A plate slid off the table and shattered on the floor. After the eruption, they heard sounds of a thunderstorm beginning toward the peak. Lightning reflected into the cave and then came thunder louder than the volcano. Adam went to the opening at the head of the stair, stared upward a few seconds, came back and sat at the table. "It's coming."

"What? What's coming?"

"I haven't told you. I wanted to be sure you were serious about leaving. At this season almost every year, there is more shaking of the mountain, then blows from the top, lava flows, streams of ash, storms around the top and heavy rain. The constant wind from the north stops—then changes. The water pulls away from the beach a little. If you go through the pass, the wind should be large in your sail. If you go, it must be soon. This Storm of Vulcan lasts about a week . . . ten days at most. Ends with a big blow at the top, streams of fire down the side and fierce winds. I sometimes go to my 'safe place.' This one sounds worse than others. You need to be clear of the island before the big blow." The next day, Job dug more channel behind the boat and held drifting sand with two sheets of plywood from the ship. He backed the boat farther into the lagoon.

At the next high tide, the three stood on the beach by the back of the boat floating in the space Job had dug. They recited the contents of the boat. Job and Ima hesitated, listened to rumbling of the volcano, and went over the list again.

Adam said, "If you go today, it must be soon; tide is beginning to go out. You need deep water to get through that pass."

Job shook Adam's hand, embraced him and said. "Goodbye friend and savior; I wish you could go with us. I try to understand. In truth, you will be with us always. We'll never forget you."

Ima hesitated, then held his arms and gave Adam a quick kiss on the cheek. Ima and Job climbed the ladder. Adam untied the rope and threw it up. Job wound the rope around the base of the mast, started the motor, backed the tender into open water, turned and headed toward the pass in the reef. Beyond the reef, he idled the engine and looked up; the sail filled and the flag streamed ahead. From the open sea, they looked back. The shrinking figure on the beach was still waving.

Higher Water

Ima watched until the mist-covered island disappeared. She said, "I can't remember my name or my home, but when you were helping him read the Bible. I remembered the stories. His name was Adam . . . have we left Eden?"

"He never gave it a name. He called it 'the island' or 'this place.' It was *an* Eden for him . . . and for us, but I don't think *the* Eden. I must admit though, we ate nothing but fruit . . . and there *was* a fruit that caused death. Everything we needed came from trees. He did name some animals. It wasn't like any place I've seen."

The wind was gentle and the water smooth. Job turned off the engine, tied the wheel and stared out to sea. Ima saw his brooding look and said, "I was concerned with my problems. I know I should have asked before; was your wife lost in the storm?"

Job looked at Ima, then the sea, and thought a long time before answering. "She was lost . . . to me in the storm. I believe she is still somewhere . . . and hope she comes back."

She rested her hand on his arm and said, "I'm sorry."

Instinctually he put his arms around her. For a moment, she seemed at home there and then pushed him away. "You promised you would respect my circumstances."

He turned and looked back at the sea.

Job warned Ima again, "Remember, always wear your life preserver and your safety line." He left the engine off, the wheel tied, accepted the wind in the small sail, and they slept.

Job woke as his head bumped against the side of the boat.

The tender was rolling and pitching; waves hitting the boat sprayed water over him. He woke Ima. She jumped up and said, "Are we back in the same storm that took us to the island?"

"No, but it's a storm. I have to climb the ladder and reef the sail. If I don't, the storm will tear it away. I tell you again, always snap your safety rope to something. The sea is ever ready to take one more." He worked his way up the ladder, moving the catch on his rope as he went. By the time he started the engine and turned the boat into the wind, the storm was violent. With controlled direction, the boat was more stable.

After hours and what seemed days, the storm passed as suddenly as it came. Job idled the engine and said. "I'm not up to another trip to the sail right now. We've learned a valuable lesson; no matter how peaceful the sea, one of us has to stay awake and watch the weather and water ahead. We can't cut through the waves; any rough water will toss us like a big pancake. If it gets bad enough, we might have to throw things over the side and cut away the raft." He looked at the rope, moving snake-like in the wake of the boat. "We're further committed. The storm took the little boat we were towing--the one I used to haul so many things. We've lost our friend, now one of our boats and all we had in it. It must have filled with water and the weight broke the rope. We must not lose anything else . . . or each other."

Job slept the sleep of exhaustion. Ima forced herself to stay awake and watch. As darkness came, she moved from side to side of the boat, rubbed her eyes and stared at the horizon. She called to Job, but did not touch him. She called several times. "I hate to wake you, but I see a speck on the horizon that might be something. Job groaned as he struggled to get up, rummaged in a bag for binoculars and looked at where Ima had pointed.

"It 's a ship."

"But it's so far away."

"It's almost dark. We'll get close as we can, while we can see." Job started the engine, turned the boat north and as the ship was about to pass, fired the flare gun. The flare hit the water with a sizzle 20 feet from the boat. The next two didn't go as far. He turned on their small lights and blinked them. The ship disappeared in the west.

"Don't cry. It's just one ship. We'll turn east in the direction that one came from and try to find others. Flares are a lost cause. Probably got wet in the storm."

The next day, a ship came close enough for them to pull alongside. They waved and shouted for help. High above them, men on the deck smiled, waved back and the ship was gone. As it steamed out of sight, Job said, "We can't pass very close. They would swamp us. They see us underway and that high up can't hear us over their engine noise. They think we wave to be friendly. There are flags to send messages, but we don't have any. We were flying a flag upside-down, but the storm took it. Maybe they'll stop when they see us out of fuel and adrift. We certainly don't have enough to take us to California."

They saw nothing but open sea for days. Job ran the engine a little each day, but tried to use the small sail most of the time and hold to the direction the ships seemed to travel. Early one day, he was watching the horizon ahead through binoculars when he felt what he thought was a puff of air at his back. He heard nothing but water against the boat. He turned and looked behind at an empty sea. Later in the day, he saw a boat, little bigger than theirs, going north. He reefed the sail and with the engine on turned to intersect them. He pulled alongside and began his story and plea for help. This tine he was heard, but the man on deck interrupted him and shouted, "Sorry we can't help. Radio says something blew up and we got a tsunami headed this way . . . don't know how bad. Must have been underwater--no land where it came from. We can't make it back to the coast. Can't make it to Hawaii either, but we hope to get to the northwest. If we're lucky, the islands will block some of the wave. If your boat will make it, you better try, too." He pulled away and never looked back. Job idled the engine and stared at the wake of the boat.

Ima said, "Will we go?"

"We are still a big pancake. I'll get as many miles behind us as I can with the sail and save fuel for the time when the wave comes. We hope and pray the miles of water weakens and slows that wave." They turned east and saw another ship, but didn't try to contact it. "Look to the southwest with the binoculars and tell me when it comes. You have to watch really close. It may not be very high. Look for something different: a long low wave. I am going to fill the tank with every ounce I can get in."

"What will we do when it comes?"

"We can't cut through it; we'll try to ride it like a big fat surfboard. Lilly pads don't turn over; maybe we won't either."

After what seemed hours taking turns watching, Ima said, "Looks like the horizon just raised up a little bit."

Job took the binoculars and saw the long wave coming. He might not have seen it but for the debris it carried. He almost ran up the rope ladder and secured the sail with extra ties. The engine turned over, but wouldn't start. On the fourth try it cranked and Job breathed again. He looked around at the coming wave. "Get in that compartment. Close everything--any opening. It's coming fast. The miles didn't slow it much. We don't know what it will do. If we go over, you have to get out. Your life preserver will hold you up, but take the snap loose on your safety line. It's a big ocean, but you can hope for rescue." Job watched the wave over one shoulder while he steered the boat and tried to keep at right angles to the wave. It was low, but seemed to come faster and faster. He had no idea what it would do and pushed the engine to its limits as the wave hit. The little boat was lifted up and then tilted nose down with the propeller racing in air. Water spilled over the boat; it became level and surged ahead. He cut back on the engine; water cleared and they were riding the wave. Job struggled with the wheel and engine to keep the boat straight. He screamed to Ima to open something for ventilation, but be ready to close it. Several times the boat turned and twisted, but straightened at the last second. After hours and what seemed an eternity, the wave began to be higher, faster, and break with froth. The mast was bent back; the sail ripped and flapped in shreds. The wind first tore away Job's hat, then his dark glasses. He had look down then squint and raise his head for a second at the time until he could reach the goggles in his pocket. They were not tinted and the glair was intense. Job still had to squint. He saw a long dark line on the horizon ahead. It couldn't possibility be another wave. It had to be land. As they got closer, he saw boats entering a river or bay. Ima could stand it no longer, came out of hiding, shielded her eyes and looked ahead for a second. She turned away and pulled at jobs sleeve, "What is that and what are we going to do?"

"The storm and this big wave have both pushed us east. That's land—I hope California and not South America. If we hit it at this speed, we'll crash. There is an opening to the left. I'm going to try to work us over there. It's our only hope. Stay down out of the wind and don't look into it. If we crash . . . always remember . . . I love you." He glanced for a second; Ima appeared startled. Her lips moved, but sounds of rushing water drowned words, if they came.

The wave they rode became even higher; they almost turned sideways at times, but the boat dropped back from the edge a little, was more level and Job had better control. As they rushed toward the open area on the shore ahead, one boat crashed into the side of another in mid-channel. Job gambled and reversed the engine for a second to drop farther back. He raced the engine forward to gain control again. There was no choice; the wave pushed him straight for the two boats. One backed out of the side of the other as the wave hit.

The one with the hole on the side tumbled over and was thrown to the left and the other swept to the right. Job had little control as the boat veered to the left between the two. In the confined space the wave seemed to move faster and they dropped back even more. When the wave hit the shore, boats and debris were thrown over the banks. Fish and other creatures of the sea were scattered at the crest of the wave. Some buildings near the shore were crushed; smaller ones exploded when the water poured in. The wave stuck the pillars of a bridge and a roadway section with a car fell. As they were swept along, floating objects struck the sides, but the thick rubber held. Far ahead, the wave struck a long pier, lifted it up, swept away a boat at the end and turned over another on the far side. The pier leaned with the water then fell back. Job waited until most of the surge with debris passed and reversed the engine. He had to repeat the process of fast forward then reverse for a second wave. After it passed, he turned the boat, slowed, let it drift to the pier, and reversed at the last second to bump the raft against the pilings. The boat rocked at the side of the pier, but Job couldn't let go of the wheel. He watched water reach a peak on the bank and drain back carrying parts of boats, houses, and people—some screaming, some with no more motion or sound than the pieces of wood floating next to them. When the level dropped to what seemed near normal, he forced his hands loose, turned off the engine, and threw two lines over pilings to secure the boat. It took several tries across the raft. Screams, shouts, crashes, and grinding sounds slowly faded. Water continued to drain from the shore, but slower.

Arrival in Disaster

Job and Ima straightened the rows of sealed containers, made sure the plants had survived, picked each up, held it over the side and washed it with some of their drinking water. Job was dipping the seawater from the bottom of the boat when he heard a voice from above. "I am glad you like my pier."

He looked up to see three men looking down.

Job dropped his bucket and stood. "I am sorry. The wave must have washed away your sign. As big as it was, I thought this was a public pier. I'll move. I'm glad

I'm not hearing those words in Spanish. We didn't know where we were."

"It's not necessary for you to move. Our building is back from the water damage. As soon as the waves fell back, we came to check on my two boats. It took us a while; we had to move things out of the road. As you can see, one boat is on her side and the other is washed away somewhere. Stay where you are. I am glad you survived the wave. You have reached California. You hear some Spanish here, but mostly English. I'm interested in your boat. First one I have ever seen with water wings. They kept you from turning over in the high water. Where did you sail from?"

"We think from the island that caused the big wave. It had a volcano that was threatening to blow when we left. I can't tell you where it is. Our cruise-ship wrecked there in a storm about a year ago. This is the tender-- with a few modifications."

"Now that you are here, what will you do?"

"Try to get across the country to home. I'm sure we were thought dead, long ago. The stay on the island changed our appearance to complicate matters. We have a lot of things to carry, so I had hoped to rent a truck. With all the damage, that may not be possible."

"These men will help you get those water wings off so you can get to the pier easier; then you better rest a little. From your words, I would guess you're from the South and that will be a long trip. I have a hotel very near. We will take you there. With this water damage, rooms will be filled everywhere."

"I have to unload the boat first, or it will sink when we take the wings off. We have packages sealed against the water and live plants from the island. They are like no other. I hope to preserve them. Those on the island may have been lost when the volcano blew."

"More foreign plants to cover our country?"

"I've considered that. These come from an island covered with mist and fog in a warm wind. When we sailed away and looked back, it seemed like a low cloud in the distance. These trees will not live without that cover and warm breezes. In this country, I don't think they'll grow outside a greenhouse."

The men hauled up the boxes with a rope, then plants and loaded both in their truck. When the boat was unloaded and the water wings collapsed, the two climbed a ladder. On the pier, Job introduced himself and Ima. If they thought her name peculiar, they didn't say. The man who spoke was Ezra Hope. He was tall, slender, probably in his late 60s His combed straight back white hair had streaks of black, making it a silver color. The other two were Bob and G. W. They were younger, short, muscular and silent. Job and Ima sat in the back seat of the crew-cab with G. W. They drove a slow winding path through destroyed neighborhoods to the hotel beyond the damage. Each time the truck bumped over debris in the road, Job turned to look at his plants through the rear window.

Ezra said, "We have a solarium. We'll put your plants there and cover them with the plastic screen you were using on the boat. We will use the vaporizer we have for our guests. We'll put all your boxes there and lock the door. Is that satisfactory?"

"It's more than satisfactory. You are truly a Good Samaritan. We would not have survived either shore we landed on, if not for a kind man who volunteered to help. All the boxes have a number so we can be sure we have them all."

Job and Ima watched placement in the solarium and took their small bundle of clothes toward the desk.

After he spoke with the desk clerk, Ezra said, "We have only one room left. It has one double bed. I see rings, are you not man and wife?"

Ima answered, "No, he was a stranger to me after the storm."

Job said. "A rollaway?"

The desk clerk said," All in use."

"How about extra sheets and comforter. I'll make a pallet on the floor. I'm not sure I can sleep, but I can clean up and rest."

"We will have extra bedding, toilet articles, something to sleep in, and sleeping pills in case you need one."

A man ushered them into a room and handed Job a key. As he left, he put the do-not-disturb sign on the doorknob. Ima began walking around the room feeling the smoothness of the furniture and softness of the bed. She said, "I didn't remember how nice things could be."

Job watched as he spread his bed on the floor. On one of her rounds, he said, "You better get in that bathroom, take your shower and get in bed before you pass out. You think you don't remember, but all those knobs and things in there will come back to you."

Job didn't lie on his bed in the floor. He was afraid he wouldn't be able to get up. He finally heard shower noise. Eventually, Ima came out dressed in pajamas much too large and a towel tied around to cover the looseness. "It's your turn, but when you come out, you don't have to sleep on the floor. I will fix the bed. You promised you would respect me. Should I take one of those pills?"

Job looked at the label of the bottle in the bathroom. He knew the drug. He handed Ima one. "I would take half; if you wake up, take the other half."

Job looked at a complete set of toilet articles provided by their benefactor. His slow shower seemed to relax some of the tightness of his muscles. In spite of the long soak of his face, shaving days and weeks growth of beard was painful. He hesitated, took a fourth of a tablet, thought again and took another fourth.

In the bedroom, Ima had rolled all of the extra bedding from the floor and placed the roll under the covers in the center of the bed, clearly marking his half. He lay down and all the tension slowly seemed to fade away. He tried not to think about how ridiculous it was to be sleeping in the same bed as his wife with a barrier between them. The roll was small compared to the amnesia. *If I could move the amnesia as easily as I could that roll…..*

A loud noise and voices woke him. It sounded as if somebody had fallen against the door or pushed something into it. *I wouldn't think this hotel would have that much noise in the middle of the night.* He suddenly realized light was streaming around blinds at the windows. Job looked at the clock. It couldn't be PM it had to be 10AM. It took several minutes of stretching to loosen muscles in his arms and legs enough to try to get up. He walked around the bed and picked up a note that had been slid under the door. It said, *Come to the dining room. New clothes are just outside the door.* His face was still tender and he shaved carefully. When he dressed, he woke Ima.

After she dressed, they left the room, walked the hall and stepped into an empty elevator. Job said, "Now listen very carefully; you must never ever say why you think we have changed."

"But I heard you talking with Adam about the little wrinkled brown fruit we eat every day."

"Yes I know, but we don't know how they worked, so I can truthfully say we can't explain how the change took place. Never mention those fruits or we have big problems."

A little after 11:00 they walked into the dining room. A waiter seated them and made a phone call. Ezra sat across the table within minutes. "I know you have eaten what you had available on the island. I saw the dried fruit you carried in the boat. I have taken the liberty of ordering your first meal. I believe it will be something your stomachs can tolerate. After they talked several minutes, one waiter set down three plates of pasta with white sauce and slivers of chicken. Another placed salads and garlic bread. Job stared at he first cooked food he had seen in a year. The aroma was almost more than he could endure. *I can hardly wait to try this, but I intend to give thanks.* He bowed his head and began. "Thank you for deliverance from the great storm, for our life on the island, for your guiding hand on the boat over the great wave, and for helping hands on both shores. We ask for your direction and help in trials we know are coming. Thank you for this food we are about to receive. In Christ's name. Amen."

They looked up to see conversation stopped at tables around them and people staring. Waiters were standing still with plates of food. Ezra said, "That may have the first time some have heard grace said in this restaurant."

"I am glad to be the first and hope I won't be the last."

After their plates were clean, Ezra said, "If you feel up to it, I would like for you to show me how your boat sails. I had new canvas put on it this morning and a little fresh diesel in the tank. I have been sailing for years, but I have never had anything quite like your boat. It's rigged like a Viking ship. I know the square sail makes it hard to tack; I don't see how you made it this far."

"You do what you have to do. I never sailed anything before; I had never even paddled a boat. We were blessed by having a professional sailor living on the island. He taught me what little I know. Without favorable winds, we wouldn't have made it. We'll never know how far the tsunami pushed us—and a storm before that. I'll go with you to the boat, but I'm not up to climbing to the yard. It takes at least two to handle the boat. It was hard for Ima to help."

"We will take both the men who helped yesterday,"
Ima said, "I will watch from the pier. I don't want to
be on that boat any more.

Ezra said, "You don't need to stand that long. We'll
park the truck where you can sit and watch. Job, I
suppose your families were glad to hear from you. I told
the man who showed you to the room to tell you to feel
free to make calls."

Job said. "We didn't call, nor will we call. Ima has
amnesia from the anguish of the storm and a head injury
from a fall; the bruise on her forehead took weeks to
fade. She doesn't know who to call or where. We have
also had changes we will never be able to explain."

Ezra said, "I can understand how isolation on an
island for a year would change you . . . others will, too."

Job pulled out his billfold. It had been soaked in the
storm and the big wave, but his driver's license was
sealed in plastic. He handed it to Ezra. He looked from
the picture in his hand to the man across the table
several times. "I see the resemblance. By the date of
birth, the man in this picture is 82. This is your father . . .
or your grandfather?"

"That is me."

"But as you sit here at this table in this year of 2009,
you could pass for 40 . . .or younger."

"I told you I couldn't explain it." Job told all he knew
about the process of aging and said, "In the year we
were on the island, we were physically changed. I can't
tell you how, but it happened to us and to the man who
was cast away on the same island many years before. I
cannot call my children and tell them not only am I
alive, but I'm younger than they are. I am physically
younger. You know an 82 year-old man couldn't make it
across the Pacific in a sailboat. When we landed on the
island, I had trouble walking on the beach. You may
have unloaded a walking stick. I brought it to remind

myself of past days. If you have trouble believing this, think of the troubles I'll have with friends and family."

Ezra looked once more at the picture and handed it back. "What you say is true; I see the picture, see your face across the table, hear your words, but don't understand. We'll look at that boat, if you are ready."

Ima sat in the truck parked by the pier and the men climbed down to the boat. Job adjusted the ropes to the yard, started the engine, backed the boat out, and turned it toward the opposite shore of the bay "Now, Bob, you or G. W. pull the ropes and let the sail fall."

He idled the engine as they did; the sail filled with a pop and the boat began moving across the water. With gusts of wind, the mast bent forward, when it straightened it seemed to give an extra push to the boat.

Job said, "You better loosen the sail at the bottom and reef it soon." He had to reverse the engine as they finished. They crossed back to the pier. "Is that enough or do you want more?"

As Ezra shook his head, Job turned off the engine. Ezra said, "That's quite enough. Tell me about the boat; what size engine does it have?"

"I have no idea; I had to take it as it was . . . whatever it was."

"And the strange mast and yard that seems flexible and the pale red paint that feels like glass?"

Job told of the source of both. "There was a small container of the liquid sap from the paint tree. You may have unloaded it with the boxes. We had some bumps to the boat, but I never used it."

Ima was standing and waiting on the pier.

* * *

As they rode back, Ezra said, "You two have to have a little hair work. Looks long overdue. We have a place in the hotel. It will be a busy day for you. Have your hair done and before your dinner, come to my office on second floor about five." He took them to the shop on the first floor.

He introduced them and left. A woman looked at Ima, pulled the ribbon letting her hair fall and said, "This will not be a problem, as young as you are, I think this dark blond hair would look best a little more than shoulder length. Even though straight, it's a little long for you to manage as it is. The wave on top helps. I have no idea what happened to the color. You have two shades of hair and for some reason a gray stripe between the two. The part toward the scalp is even colored. The long end is faded looking with streaks of gray. I'll try to correct the color, trim a little, shape it, and you will be through . . . unless you want something else? I see you wear no makeup. Your skin is smooth and almost glows. Your lips are full. With your green eyes, you have lots of color. If you do use makeup, use very little." Ima said nothing, but nodded.

The beautician asked Job, "Do you want to keep your long hair? You have lots of gray, but it's on the very ends of the hair. I can cut above that and shape it or I could color correct it and let it grow and you could have a ponytail."

"I want a flattop."

"That is a problem. I don't do flattops. A man who works here does. He will be back shortly."

The barber had a hard time making Job's hair stand up after a year lying flat. He gave him a can of spray to retrain his hair.

Job's gray was gone, but for sprinkles at the temples; the rest was brown and matched his eyes. Ima appeared startled at the change, but there was no recognition in her eyes. Job saw Ima as the woman he remembered from so many years ago and could not help staring and wanting to touch her.

The two in the shop refused money and said it had been taken care of.

* * *

They knocked on the door of the office a few minutes before five. Ezra opened it and said, "I think your time in the salon well spent. You have dropped more years. Now you are into the 30's. You don't look like you just crossed the Pacific in a sailboat. Job, I hope you never have to use that driver's license." He introduced the man across the desk, "This is my attorney. He has documents I want you to consider." All four sat and the attorney picked up one of the papers. "This says you, Ira Lee Jobson, Sr. took possession of the boat and the contents of the ship after the storm and wreck. You claim ownership by right of salvage. The tender and items from the ship now belong to you. Read it and if you agree, we will call another witness and you can sign. You get one copy."

After the paper was signed and notarized, the attorney picked up another. "This one says you transfer ownership of your boat to Ezra."

Ezra said, "I have been sailing for years. My boats are on the bottom of the bay or ruined. I want your boat . . . it's like nothing I have ever had. The sail is so big for that small mast." Job opened his mouth to say something, but Ezra held up his hand and stopped him. "There is more; in the morning you will have your plants and boxes loaded on a truck. There will be a mist generator and a shield for the plants. I have marked a map to get you across the county. I have routed you around a couple of state lines where you might be inspected. I believe your story about the plants, but they wouldn't."

Job wiped his eye with a knuckle. "You must have had somebody show you great kindness in the past for you to do something like this." He signed the paper without reading it.

Land Cruise

Early the next morning, they stood around a new truck in front of the hotel. It was a little higher than most because of the four-wheel drive. It had a shell over a straight side short bed. Plants were in rows in a compartment in front of the tailgate. The tinted plastic covering for the plants was not visible from the side or back. Boxes were in the front and accessible through a locked door on each side of the shell. A tube carried air from the cab. A vaporizer added a mist. Job could control the tube of air for the plants, according to the temperature of the compartment. The gauge was taped to the central hump in the floor. Ezra said, "Best we could do on short notice."

"I marvel that you did all this. You have my water born Ark and have given me a land born Ark."

Ezra said, "You were right about kindness shown to me. I lost my entire family and home in a storm that blew in from the coast. Times were hard and neighbors couldn't help, so after the funerals I took what little money I had and went toward this city . . . walking . . . trying to find work, but nobody was interested in a skinny fourteen-year-old kid. A bunch of toughs beat me, took what little I had and left me at the side of the road. A man came by and took me to his home. He and his wife had no children. I lived with him until I finished school and then went to work for him. His wife died and years later when he died, he left his estate to me. Yes, I have tried to show kindness to people in need. I may have done more for you than others. You had the strangest story and the greatest need, but I can never repay the debt I owe. Here is a little gas money." He handed Job an envelope. "My phone number is written there and here is my card. Here is the receipt for the truck, receipt for the tag, and insurance papers. When the title comes, I'll send it—when you tell me where to send it. The address listed on everything is my office on the second floor of the hotel. I can't help you with the driver's license. Is there anything else you need?"

"You have thought of everything. It's been a year since I've driven. I will be a little slow getting out of town"

"One man will follow in my truck; the other will drive you to the edge of town, then you drive until it all comes back. When you feel comfortable, stop again, let him out and my truck will pick him up." He offered his hand, "You will make it."

Job took his hand and pulled him forward and put his arms around him. "Thank you more than you will ever know. I'll call you when or if I can get my life back and if Ima can find herself." Ima held his arms and gave him a quick kiss on the cheek. As they drove away, Ezra waved like Adam did until they were out of sight. They ate some of their dried fruit when they stopped for gas. A little before dark Job said, "We have a long way to go, but I have had about all I can take on this first day. They ate at the motel and went to their room. Ima still wanted one room and one bed. She insisted Job shower first. When he finished, there was a roll of bedding dividing sides of the bed as before. He never remembered her coming to bed.

After coffeecake and water, they were on the road again. They tried coffee, but after a year, couldn't tolerate the taste. At every stop, Job checked their plants and boxes. He drove a little longer the second day. Job had to shower first again. This was washday. He hung his on an empty towel rack. Ima hid her underwear in the shower to dry. The next morning, Job tried to tell her that was not a good place to dry things. She pretended not to hear.

They drove even farther the third day. Most of the stress from the ride on the big wave was fading and Job was becoming accustomed to driving again. On the water, threat of death was a wave away; on the highway, death rushed past inches away. He drove a little below the speed limit, but that still meant the vehicles on a two lane road passed each other at 130 miles an hour.

After they ate the next night, they began the routine of showers. Job insisted that it was her time to go first. She left the door partly open. Job saw her image in the mirror as she got out of the shower. She was slimmer; curves were greater, as he remembered from years ago. He turned his head. After his shower, he stopped to look at the sleeping pills Ezra had furnished, ignored them and went to the bedroom. The dividing roll was in place and Ima was on one side. She was still and breathing slowly. Job watched her sleep by the bathroom light several minutes before he turned it off. He lay on his side of the bed and stared into darkness. *How ridiculous this is. I can see her and hear what little she says, but can't hold her hand . . . or touch her.... and yet . . . she's my wife. Maybe I can reach under that barrier roll and touch her arm just to know she's there.* Job moved very slowly.

As soon as he felt skin, she moved away and said, "Stop that! You promised you wouldn't . . . several times. You know I don't know who I belong to."

Job jerked his hand back. "Sorry, I must have rolled over in my sleep. I'll move over a little." He got up, went to the bathroom, splashed cold water in his face and looked in the mirror. His wrinkles were gone, drooping cheeks were tight, most of his hair was brown, but memories and hormones were surging. By the light of the bathroom, Job walked back to the other room, pulled out the drawer of the bedside table, took out the book, and sat on the side of the bed. He looked for several minutes before he found the passage and then read it twice.

If I speak with the tongues of men and of angels, but do not have love, I have become a noisy gong or a clanging cymbal.

And if I have the gift of prophesy, and know all mysteries and all knowledge; and if I have all faith so as to remove mountains, but do not have love, I am nothing.

And if I give all of my possessions to feed the poor, and if I deliver my body to be burned and do not have love, it profits me nothing.

Love is patient, love is kind and is not jealous; it does not brag, and is not arrogant,

does not act unbecomingly; it does not seek its own, it is not provoked, does not take into account a wrong suffered,

does not rejoice in unrighteousness, but rejoices with the truth,

bears all things, believes all things, hopes all things, endures all things.

Love never fails; but if there are gifts of prophesy, hey will be done away; if there are tongues, they will cease; if there is knowledge, it will be done away.

For we know in part, and we prophesy in part; but when the perfect comes, the partial will be done away.

When I was a child, I used to speak as a child, think as a child, reason as a child; when I became a man, I did away with childish things.

For now we see in a mirror dimly, but then face to face; now I know in part, bu then I shall know fully just as I am fully known

But now abide faith, hope, love, these three; but the greatest of these is love.[1]

He closed the book, stared at the wall and thought on these strange circumstances. *It says love never fails, but I need strength. I can do nothing, but remember the love she had for me and hope it's still inside . . . somewhere. But will it ever come back?* He put the book down and stood a calmer man, but still went back to the bathroom and took a whole sleeping pill.

---

[1] 1 Corinthians 13, NAS

As they left the room the next morning, Ima picked up the newspaper at the door, folded it and took it to the breakfast table. She opened it when they sat in the truck. "Here is a picture of our island on page three--or what's left of it." She gave the paper to Job.

He scanned the article and looked at the picture a long time. "The top of the mountain and part of the slopes are gone, but looks like lava flows and ash are building it again. Too much fog and mist to see that big rock where the cave is . . . or was. They say the volcano blow caused the earthquake to make the big wave like we thought. They advise ships to avoid the area. With all the fog and steam, from a distance the island still looks like a low cloud."

"What do you think happened to Adam?"

"If that old--as Adam called it--mountain with a fire in its throat gave warning, he was in his 'safe place.' If he didn't get there, the blast from the volcano got him. He wasn't afraid of dying. He thought his work was done, but I hope the fire didn't pour over him. That was his greatest fear."

Job pulled out of the parking lot and onto the highway. After a half hour of silence, Ima said, "I am sorry if I was abrupt and rude last night, but nothing must go on between us. I am attracted to you, but I have to remember I don't know whose wife I am. I know you could have lied to me and said you were my husband. Thank you for respecting my dilemma."

Job took a quick look at Ima. She was at the point of tears. *This gets crazier and crazier; I've considered trying to tell her the truth and now I can't.*

Job said, "First big city we come to, we need to stop and get X-rays and studies on your head. You might have damage from the fall you took."

"No, we have waited a year, we can wait until you see your family and prove you aren't dead. At least you know where to go. Besides, I saw my mother yesterday."

"You *what, where,* in a town we passed through or the motel? You didn't tell me." *This couldn't be. Her mother has been dead for years.*

"Not the real person; I suddenly saw her in my mind . . . my memory. At least, I think it was my mother. I walked home from school, went to the kitchen and sat at the table. I wish she had called me by name, but she didn't. But I think memories like that are like dreams; you may know what somebody says, but you don't hear real sounds or words. Maybe my memory is coming back"

"Any return is a good sign. It could come little at the time or all at once. I still say, at some stage we have to have studies done to see what damage the fall did to your head."

Home For One

After days of travel, one afternoon they turned off the highway. Job glanced at Ima. She didn't seem to recognize familiar signs. The day before, she hadn't noticed when they crossed the line into Alabama.

He drove past his rental properties, his old office and last of all, their home of many years. Some yards were not mowed and 'For Sale' signs were in front of two buildings. Ima showed nothing.

After Job slowed to look several times, Ima said, "This is your hometown?"

"Yes, this is New Canaan."

"Now what?"

"We go to a motel as usual, then we have to find a place for the plants to live, while I try to get my life back."

After they were settled in a room, he called a realty company he had never done business with before. The agent said this was an unusual request, but he would check and call back.

The agent called the next morning to say he had one property with a greenhouse, but the dwelling was small and a second house was even smaller. Job borrowed tools from the maintenance man and opened box # 1 from the back of the truck

They drove the truck; the plants needed cooling and ventilation. The man living in the smaller house was waiting. He was a short muscular man with gray hair and leather like hands with broken nails. Job asked Billy Joe Scraggs to give the history. He said, "The owner was agona get in the plant business in a big way, and hired me full time. His wife died out and he taken to the bottle real bad. His son put him in some sorta home, got control of his money, got rid of th' plants and put this place up fa' sale. He lets me stay here, but I haveta live off odd jobs."

The greenhouse had a sprinkler system, was tall enough and tight enough. Billy Joe's house was three rooms and a bath, but neat and clean. The other house was slightly bigger, but the inside looked and smelled little better than the edge of a landfill.

The realtor came while they were looking at the larger house. He said, "They're not hooked up now, but it has available power, water, and phone."

Job said, "But no garbage pickup. Can you make arrangements to clean out this mess, paint the walls and ceiling and put tile on this floor . . . and soon?"

"I think so."

He said to Billy Joe, "Do you know where to get materials to change that greenhouse?"

"Yes, I've worked on 'em and in 'em most of my life."

"And how long has this place been on the market"

The realtor said, "Uh . . . ah . . . about eight months . . . maybe twelve or so."

Job stared at the structures and said, "Offer $20,000 less than he's asking."

The realtor came to the motel room that afternoon. "He will take your offer. He's signed the papers, but he wants a down payment now."

"How much?"

"About $5,000 should be adequate."

Job pulled out a package from his pocket and began counting out bills.

"Wait a minute; write me a check. I can't go across the parking lot with that kinda money."

Job kept counting, "You said $5,000 and here it is-- good American money. I don't have a checking account; you'll have to take real money and I do want a receipt." The realtor called a man from his office to take him to the bank.

After he left, Ima said, "Why haven't you called your family?"

"I suppose I was afraid to. I'll try while we wait on our house."

The oldest son was at work, so he called his daughter. He got the disbelief he expected. She would not allow him to come to her home, but agreed to see him in a restaurant at four that afternoon.

Ima stayed in the truck. Another jolt to their children's world would be too much. His daughter Sarah was not alone. Her husband and Ira, Jr. were there. Job pulled up a chair so he could face them in the booth. He looked from one to the other, smiled and began. "First, tell me about your children . . . and grandchildren." Sarah's husband turned his head and tried to withdraw from the confrontation. Job's two children stared and said nothing. "Sarah, I told you a year on that island changed me. I can't explain it, but it happened. I have my old drivers license, house keys, and Army dog tags." He laid them on the table. "I thought about my family every day I was gone and could hardly wait to see you." They looked at Job with a vacant stare and didn't even glance at the table. "I can tell you things from your childhood others wouldn't know. I know your children's names and can put names on their faces. Try to remember my old pictures. Close your eyes, hear my words and see my face from your childhood. I don't look the age you remember, but I am your father."

Sarah said, "We have already talked about it. You are an imposter. In some way, you got all this information and those things on the table. You decided you looked like our dad did 50 years ago and came for the money. If you are alive, where is our mother? She was on that ship, too. Our dad and mother were lost when their ship went down. The will was probated months ago. We have the estate now. Our out of town brother agrees. In case you didn't find out—his name is Josh. I talked to him by phone. An 82-year-old man can't show up looking 30 after a year of being nowhere."

Job looked from one face to the other. Ira, Jr. had more gray hair scattered through brown than he remembered. Sarah's was the same, but Job knew she had used color for years. Her scowl may have had a few more wrinkles. Both had an increasingly harsh sour look. Job said, "Because you have never seen something happen or when you do see it, you don't believe it because you didn't expect it and don't understand it, doesn't mean it can't be true. I hope it's poor judgment and not greed that blinds you and keeps you from hearing your father's voice. Everything I owned and my love were for you when I was dead . . . look at me, I'm still very much alive." He picked up the things from the table and walked away without looking back.

Job pulled out of the parking lot without a word. Ima said, "So what happened? You weren't in there long."

"What I was afraid of, but hoped wouldn't happen--total rejection."

"What will you do now?"

"I've lost the try at family, now I'll try the legal route."

He got a prompt appointment with the lawyer he had used for years. When Job walked in the office, the lawyer had a startled expression and said, "You are not who I expected; my secretary said Ira Sr. You must be Ira Jr. . . . or Ira III?" They sat and Job tried to explain the strange circumstances. The man across the desk watched while Job began and then turned his head to stare at the wall of books. He interrupted not halfway through the story. "I run a respectable law practice. I have done work for families for years. I can't be involved in some farfetched claim I don't believe. Good day . . . whoever you are."

"If you aren't willing to listen to my problems, could you at least give me information? Who is the lawyer newest in town and practicing alone?"

The attorney picked up the phone book, wrote on a note pad, tore off the sheet and handed it across the desk. "Here is his name and number, but I'm not sure even he is desperate enough to take something this weird."

As they left the parking lot Ima said, "You look down . . . more bad news?"

"People do judge a book by the cover. I know it's a stretch to believe what I'm asking, but he wouldn't listen. If people would hear my words long enough, they would know this is me inside a shell they didn't expect. Because they have never seen anything like an old man in a young body, they don't believe it can be. I have to figure something they can see from the world they know . . . something that seems logical to them."

In his life before the island, Job had known the Chief of Police and the Sheriff. The answers from both were almost identical. "That's the most ridiculous request I've ever heard. I knew Ira Jobson, and you're not him. I don't know what kind of a scam you're trying to pull. Job was a good 50 years older than you are. Nobody can turn the calendar that far back."

He left rejected again. *Maybe I should go some place where nobody ever knew me in my other life.*

He first checked on the house repairs and the greenhouse changes. The base of the lower sides of the greenhouse were now a fog shade of gray, the overhead filter was in place, the mist system and fans were working, sprinkler system installed, and gas heaters were there for the weather to come. He moved the plants and repotted them. They all suffered some damage from saltwater on the long trip. The green-fruited plants were dying, but they were never very vigorous or an important food source. The others would survive. The three-room house had been cleaned and painted. It was small, but temporarily adequate and far more convenient than having to leave the motel room several times a day to check the back of the truck and sometimes run the motor.

He bought a minimum of cheap furniture: a bed, a table for the phone in the bedroom, two chairs, a small table, two lamps for the living room, two chairs, a table, a small refrigerator, microwave, and hotplate for the kitchen. Ima couldn't remember how to cook or didn't have the confidence to try. He checked the stack of bills taken from the ship's safe. They were fading rapidly.

He drove 40 miles to the police station of the largest town in Adams County and waited his turn in an office to see the Chief. He didn't remember the man's name as an old patient. This time, Ima didn't have to wait in the truck. His request was simple; he wanted to be identified. "Please fingerprint me and get the FBI to give what information they have, make a photograph of me, certify that the picture matches the identification, then laminate them together." The Chief looked confused. "I know it's a peculiar request. What is the charge?"

"Oh . . . fifty, I guess."

He still seemed hesitant. "Don't you still have a Police Benevolent Association?"

"Uh . . . yes we do."

"Then, I make a contribution." He laid down a hundred dollar bill by the fifty.

"You need a receipt?"

"For fingerprinting charge."

When Job went back for his document, the Chief picked up a paper and said, "There must have been a mistake somewhere. I sent for confirmation and they sent the same report. This says you are 82 and were in the army a few months in '45 and '46--serial number...."

Job rattled off the number and handed him his dog tags. "Chief, things are not always what they seem. I have undergone a tremendous change; I think a change for the better, but nobody believes me or even listens. They don't hear the man within; they judge by what they see and compare it to what they expect to see. Look at the report and believe it. There will be a lawsuit. I won't call you as a witness unless I have to. I promise to keep it to a minimum. Please put the prints, the note from the FBI, your statement, and my photograph together and laminate them so I can't make changes."

"I can't do something that big here."

"I will cover the cost. If you can do it now, I'll wait."

He got a prompt appointment with the new attorney. His secretary said, "He's just finishing up with some paper work." As soon as Ima and Job sat in the empty office, she said, "You can go in now." She went to the doorway. "This is Ima Who and Ira Jobson. Ms. Who and Mr. Jobson, this is Mr. Benjamin Young." As they walked in, the man at the desk was arranging papers that appeared mostly blank. He stood to shake hands. He was small, pale, and blond with a ready smile.

"Please call me Ben. Sit down and tell me the nature of your legal problem?"

Job said, "I have a problem you or nobody else has seen. What I am about to tell you is true, though it sounds like a fairytale. Please don't reject me until I tell the whole story. I will pay for your time, even if you choose to not take such a weird case. A little over a year ago, I was thinking of stopping work. Yes, as old as I was, I still worked. A half-century habit is hard to break. You heard right. I did say half-century. We took a cruise to see how I would tolerate time off. We didn't know how small the ship was until we saw it at the dock. In a violent storm, the ship wrecked near an uncharted island. We were the only survivors. We lived there a year with the help of a man who had been alone on the island many years. He wouldn't say how long, but had never seen a flashlight before. Something happened to us on that strange island covered with mist from a volcano and fog from the sea. Something put every cell in our body in reverse. It's the dream of every old man to have knowledge and wisdom of age with the strength of youth. Part of my dream became a nightmare. A terrible event in a man's life can make him look years older. People may be startled by the change, but they accept it. They don't believe the opposite. You can move forward in aging, but not back. That's why I'm here. That's why I'm here. I do have some proof." He handed Mr. Young his driver's license.

"This says the driver is 82."

"I am the driver. That is my true age. Here's the log of the ship and further proof of identity." He laid on the desk the laminated prints, photograph, and FBI identification.

Mr. Young picked them up and looked at each several times. "Even if this . . . this wild story is true, I don't understand what I can do."

"Our ship was lost and thought sunk. I called the cruise line office the day after we got to the coast. The ship lost all contact with the rest of the world in the middle of the storm. Some bodies were later recovered and the rest of the crew and passengers thought dead. My family rejects me; they have taken everything I owned. I see all I have worked a lifetime to accumulate being neglected or sold. My home and office are empty and locked. All of this was for my family eventually, but not just yet. I would like to have these things a few more years. I cannot practice medicine because my licenses and my insurance contacts are gone. I have no liability insurance. I am officially a dead man. I have no identity. I am lost to genealogy. I exist as a generic being. I never realized how life would be with no family at all. You can't force my children to accept me, but in some way I would like to have part of my life back. The cruise and year on the island did tell me what I wanted to do. I was doing a limited practice. Now that I am stronger, I may want to do more surgery, but to work, I must exist as a real person."

Mr. Young stared at Job, then the objects on the desk and said, "Please excuse me while I make a call." He opened a drawer, pulled out a little notebook, looked up a number, made the call, turned toward the wall, and waited a few minutes. After words of greeting, suggesting this call was to a professor or an older colleague, he told Job's story. Then he said, " No, this is not a joke. I am serious. When I first heard it, I didn't believe it either. I have the fingerprints and the ID from the FBI on my desk." He stopped and listened a long time, then said, "I see, thank you very much. I believe I can do that. Yes, I realize it's a strange story and a real gamble for me, but as you told us, much of life is a gamble. I'll tell you how it comes out."

He turned his chair toward the desk, moved the things Job had brought and stared at each. He looked up at the two across the desk. "We can file for Declaratory Judgment in Circuit Court. I will send the papers to the Court Clerk as soon as I can. Your children will be the defendants. After your children are notified by the court, their attorney has 30 days to respond."

"I must sue my own children?"

"They are the ones who claimed your death, probated your will, took your estate, and now don't believe you inhabit a young body. You are the plaintiff and they are defendants. In their defense, I must say, it's hard for me to accept. We have to understand; the world will think us crazy . . . until they see the evidence. This is an effort of desperation for you, but a risk and gamble for me."

Job said, "And after the 30 days, when do we get our day in court?"

"If we are lucky, six months."

Job stared at Ben Young a full minute, turned to look at Ima, then at the floor.

"Is there a problem?"

"Many problems, but the main one is what we will do and how we will live for six months with no job, no identity, and no income."

"I can understand and identify with that thought."

'I could work for some Doc-In-a-Box place, but I have no credentials that anybody would believe. I can't even fry hamburgers. My social security number belongs to a dead man. Please proceed with the lawsuit; I need my life back . . . or at least part of it. I'll work out my other problems some way."

"What about Ms. Who? She has said nothing and you have said nothing about her. Is she just a spectator?"

Job said, "She must be completely left out of this. She has a worse identity problem than I do. She has almost total amnesia. For now she is just a spectator. She can't have any more stress."

"Now I hate to mention it, but I have to talk about my charges. I will charge hourly rates. I have no idea what the total will be."

"I understand; I came prepared to pay some in advance." He walked across the room and put ten hundred dollar bills on the desk. "Since we are new to each other, I would like a receipt."

Mr. Young appeared startled and said, "Out of curiosity, how are you living now--without income? How did you get across the country?"

"A man on the coast took our boat and gave us a truck. The bills on your desk came from the ship's safe. I was told the boat and things in the ship were mine by right of salvage. I might owe tax, but how can a dead man pay tax?"

A month later, the response from the defendants' lawyer came. It called Job's claim frivolous and impossible. Fall came early. Leaves showed their fantastic range of colors only a few days before a hard freeze and windstorm took them. Now deciduous trees were bare limbs in the cold wind and fog. The waiting began to tell on Job and Ima. After a year on the island, they had forgotten how dreary and dark cold weather could be in northeast Alabama. Job checked on the plants several times a day and planted seeds from the island.

Trip of Desperation

One afternoon, Job brought in #3 and #5 boxes from the truck, used a chisel and shears, split the side of one, took out one of Adam's rocks and held it up to the light. He opened the other box and looked at another rock. He counted the remaining bills, made several phone calls and sat staring at the wall for nearly an hour. Job moved his chair to face Ima and interrupted her reading. "I know you feel safe with me in sight and I would like to be near you, but we have a crisis. Our lawsuit is months away and we will run out of money soon. We'll have fruit on our plants, but when? We didn't ask Adam how long it would take for them to bloom. Life here is not like on the island. The trees may not grow the same. It could take years. Even if we had food, there is the power bill, phone bill, gas bill, and others. Life here is not like we knew on the island. Things were free there. All we had to do is find them. I don't know how Adam knew or if he knew, but I believe these rocks we brought are gem stones."

"You mean like rubies and emeralds?"

"Yes, I don't know what kind, but I think they are gems. I've called several in the business. Nobody around here can look at them and tell. I have made a few other calls. There are big jewelry stores in New York . . . and people who cut stones."

"Then are we going?"

"That's the problem. We can't fly. Even if we had the money, we have no believable photo ID. I don't want to drive. We still have some boxes stored in the back of the truck and I don't have money for gas and motels. There is just enough left for a round trip ticket by bus . . . for one. Could you possibly stay alone long enough for me to see if I can sell some of these stones? Looks like that's our only hope."

"That's a long trip on a bus."

"The question is: can you live with it? I can buy food for several days. I'll ask the couple in the little house to check on you. If it will make you feel any better, I'll put out a pistol I found on the ship; just don't shoot any friends. Can you do it? I wouldn't ask if I could think of any other way."

"If there is no other way, I will have to do it."

The next day, Job brought in a small TV, straightened an old antenna on the roof and hooked it up. He showed the operation to Ima.

"You shouldn't have wasted money on this. You might need it in New York."

"It's the only thing I could think of to occupy your time. I have left a stack of envelopes for you. I can't call you, but I have written a letter for each day I'm gone. Open them according to the day of the month and day of the week written on the front." He packed a few clothes, loaded a few stones and found his old walking stick behind the boxes in the truck.

* * *

The next morning, Billy Joe drove him, his small satchel, and his stick to the station and he began the long trip. Job stared at the back of the seat in front of him and thought through his plans over and over. He slept through hours of the monotonous hum of the motor. One connection was canceled because of bad weather. This delay would put him New York almost a day late. His appointment was two hours after scheduled arrival. The last bus did make it on time. He did a quick sponge bath, shaved and changed shirts in the men's room. Job asked directions at the information counter. The store was 15 blocks north. He walked toward the door and came back. "Ma'am, the sky is gray and almost black; there is no hope of seeing the sun even if the buildings were gone. I have no idea which way north is. Could you tell me so I don't have to walk to the corner and read the sign?"

"Turn left as you leave. The store you want is on the opposite side of the street."

He ignored her comment about Southerners and said "Thank you."

He walked fast because of the time, the wind, and morning chill. There were patches of dirty snow by curbs and in corners near buildings. Even at this early hour, streets were filled with people. They rushed past with coat collars pulled up around a face with no expression. Job felt invisible until somebody bumped him and he heard a mumbled sound that could have been a curse. Job couldn't tell, because so many voices were not English. He pretended to need the stick, but it made no difference. A few stepped on it. He tucked it under his arm, held his satchel close, and tried to offer a smaller target. He was in the store ten minutes before the appointment time, but had to sit and wait in an empty office.

As his breathing slowed, he forced himself to stay awake and held one of the stones in his hand. He heard heavy footsteps coming down the hall and a secretary say, "He is in your office, sir."

Job stood. The door swung open and hit the doorstop. "You are Mr. Jobson?"

Job stood. "Yes, I have come a long way to speak to you about something you should be interested in."

The man sat behind the desk and said, "I can give you a few minutes. What do you have?"

"This." Job handed him one of the smaller rocks and sat in the chair in front of the desk.

The man glanced at it. "I can tell by the color, it is dyed or stained. You have wasted your time and mine. We don't have them in our store."

"That is not a dyed stone. It's in its natural state. Have it cut and see."

He picked up visor-loops, fitted then on his head, and looked more carefully. He punched a button on his desk and said, "Have Smith and Barns come in here." He didn't look up, but said, "You have more of these? Where did you get them?"

"To your first question: yes I do. To the second: I got them honestly."

The other men came in without speaking, pulled up chairs from along the wall, sat at the side of the desk, looked at the stone and stared at Job.

"You say you have not stained the stone. We can have a quick machine cut and see." He punched the button again. "Have one of our cutters come in." About 15 minutes later, there was a knock on the door. A small slightly stooped man about 50 came in. "I was making a delivery here and they said you wanted one of us."

"Look at this . . . this rock and see if it is worth our time."

He pulled out jeweler's loops from his pocket, rotated out one of the lenses and looked at the stone. "It appears to be a gemstone. If it is a diamond, it is a shade I have not seen. To do the best job, we need several hours. I could have a machine cut by afternoon, but it will not look as good."

"Get right on it the quickest way and be back right after lunch; that is all the time we can spare at this season. We will see you back here then, Mr. Jobson."

On the street, Job wrapped his head and ears with one or the strips Adam used on his legs when they climbed the slope on the island. When the wind turned bitter cold, he pretended to shop inside a store to get warm. As he left, security stopped him to check his bag. He was in the empty office when the cutter came in. "I am sorry they wouldn't let me hand work this stone. I didn't do it justice."

The two who sat at the side of the desk came first and said nothing. Then the somber man came back and sat behind the desk after a mumbled word of greeting. He was heavyset and without expression. He never introduced himself, but Job heard the secretary call him Mr. Flint. "Well, is it stained or not?"

The cutter said, "It is not a stained stone. It is a color you probably have not seen in this store. It is a diamond. I checked hardness and heat transmission." He picked up the stone with a clamp and handed it across the desk to Mr. Flint. All three passed the stone around and looked through loops. This time they hunched over and used jewelers loops held close to the stone and eye for greater magnification. Mr. Flint rocked in his chair behind the desk, looked at the other somber men, then at Job and his small satchel. "Mr. Jobson, we will pay a standard amount for rough stones and that is all you can expect for this or any others, whatever color they might be." He handed across a sheet of sizes and prices. "Most of the cost is in the cutting and presentation. This stone is ours because we cut it. We will only pay for that rough rock you brought in."

Job stared at the silent men. The cutter said, "Pardon me, I would like to say something. You pay what I charge and that has not come to pass. It was an honor for me to cut this stone. I've never seen anything quite like it. It is not a canary, it's deeper–a gold or orange -- that not only sparkles, but seems to glow from within. I charge nothing for the work. The stone and chips belong to Mr. Jobson."

The man behind the desk glared at the cutter and said, "You forget your place."

Mr. Flint reached for the stone, but was too late. Job leaned over the desk and picked up the clamp holding the stone and the box of chips. He dropped the diamond in the box and handed the clamp to the cutter. He shook his head and said, "Keep it; you don't need to pick up a stone like that with your fingers."

Mr. Flint frowned at the cutter, "You may leave. We will deal with Mr. Jobson alone. You have said quite enough."

When the door closed, he said, "We have made a fair offer to buy wherever you have at a standard price for raw stones. This is the list of prices we will pay according to size. Just because you have raw diamonds doesn't mean you can buy groceries with them . . . or a clean shirt."

Job said, "I have the only supply of these stones in the world. I came here first because I was told you were the best. I know the way I came in. I can find my way out." He put the box in his pocket, picked up his satchel and stick, walked out without looking back or answering shouted words.

Back in the cold wind outside the door, he stood at the curb and looked at the increasing crowds of rushing people. A few flakes of snow swirled in the wind. He didn't notice the uniformed policeman until he spoke. "Are ya lost, fella?"

"I may be, but not the way you think. I made a long trip to this store because I was told it was number one. Things didn't work out. Is number two anywhere close?"

The officer thought a minute. "I would say . . . number two is across town, but probably number three is about 12 blocks south."

Job groaned, "I know the way. To get here, I walked 15 north this morning. I can't hire a taxi. Don't think I can make it on foot by dark."

The officer stared at Job and then knocked on the window of a parked car. As the window came down, he said, "Say Mac, the two of you are sitting there watching the world go by; I have a man here from out of town who has a real emergency. Can't you take him a few blocks? He will never make in it this crowd. Listen to him say a few words and you know he is from far off."

There was a growl from the front seat of the unmarked car, "We are not a delivery service. We aren't supposed to do things like that."

"Come on, remember the season. I won't tell anyone you showed a little kindness under that tough skin." He told the name of the store and said, "I'll watch this corner for bank robbers until you get back." He opened the back door.

As Job got in the back seat, he said to the policeman, "Thank you. You just made me feel a lot better about this big place."

The men in the front seat said nothing in the ride. After weaving through heavy traffic several minutes, the driver slowed and stopped. Without turning his head, the other man stuck a thumb toward a store and said, "There it is."

Job said, 'Thank you for the ride," He barely got out and was closing the door, when the driver gunned the motor and pulled into a break in traffic. In the store, he told the story of the trip from Alabama, the cut stone and the low offer to buy. He had to tell it several times. He finally made it to an office with a man behind a desk He pulled out the box, held the stone with the clamp, and handed it across a desk to Mr. George Fair. Like before, others were called. They were more open in admiration of the stone. "Your competitor was so unreasonable, I never showed the other." He handed them one of Adam's rocks from the second box.

"This is a green color. That is usually surface only."

"We will never know 'til we cut it."

"Let's talk about the gold colored stone first; we need to test it to see if it is diamond."

"This man says it is." Job handed the card he found in the box.

"Solomon Goldstein . . . he is headman of a group of cutters. I don't think he would work for us."

"Try him. Call and tell him about the green stone." The men left. Job sat in the empty office and tried to stay awake.

The cutter was at the store in a half hour. He came into the office and identified his work on the yellow diamond; Mr. Fair handed him the second stone. Mr. Goldstein looked several minutes, put the stone and loops down and said, "This is a deeper green than I have seen in a diamond. It may not be surface color only. I don't want to machine cut like I did the gold one. I can take it to our place, begin today and finish in the morning. I will try to be here between eleven and twelve. I will call if there is a delay. Will that be satisfactory?" The men nodded and he left with the green stone.

Job walked out of the office slowly; he didn't notice the cutter in the hall until he spoke. "When have you slept, Mr. Jobson?"

"I slept on the bus . . . and one night in a bus station."

"When have you eaten?"

"I got something from a vendor earlier today."

"We have no children at home and a pull out sofa bed. I will call my wife. With her approval, would you accept dinner and a bed for the night? Our diet might be a little different."

They stopped at a building without windows. Mr. Goldstein said, "May I also have the gold stone and chips? I want to do some work with them."

Job handed the box. "It's all I have, but a ticket back to Alabama."

He took the box and the green stone into the building. As they left Mr. Goldstein said, "They will begin and do the rough work. I will start early in the morning and do the finishing."

They walked up two flights of stairs in a building that looked like all the others to Job. They opened the door to an old three-room apartment, but neat and clean. A woman stood just inside the door. The cutter said, "This is my wife Molly . . . and yes, some do call us Sol and Mol. She likes her real name. I don't have the wisdom and riches of the real Solomon. Sol is fine with me. Molly, this is the man I told you about: Mr. Ira Jobson,"

"Greetings from our home, Mr. Jobson. Dinner will be about a half hour. Would you like to shower before we eat?"

"I would like that and you would appreciate it, too."

After his shower, Job put on the least rumpled clothes he could find and sat at the table.

Sol said, "Will you take wine?"

Job said, "It's been a long time since I've had wine. I'll have a half glass after some food. I am afraid more would put me to sleep.

Sol looked toward his plate and said words Job didn't understand, looked up and said, "As our guest would you give thanks?"

Job bowed his head, was silent for a time and began, "Our father, forgive us for not remembering, wherever we go, you are already there and you know our needs before we do. You care for us in ways we never expected. Thank you for kindness of those you have placed in our path. Thank you for the food before us. In our Father's name, Amen."

After Job finished a second helping, they moved to the living room to talk. He covered his yawn with his hand, but couldn't hide his heavy lids. Sol said, "You are sitting on what will be your bed. We all need to retire soon. I will leave very early to finish my work and then pick you up on the way to the store."

Job woke as stiff and sore as when he fought the big wave. He slowly realized he was hearing distant sirens, horns, and roaring cars. He remembered hearing these street noises only seconds when he lay down the night before. While he slept, his shirts and a pair of cotton pants had been washed, dried, and ironed. As he was finishing his late breakfast, Mr. Goldstein called and asked him to be waiting at the street level door.

They sat across the desk a few minutes before eleven. The others came a little after the hour. Mr. Goldstein said, "I hope you are as pleased with the stones as I am.

The green one is also a diamond and an even deep green throughout. I reworked the stone from yesterday. We used a few of the larger chips of both to make stones for earrings. They are small, but with the glow and deep color, I thought then adequate." He spread a cloth on the desk and laid out the yellow stone from the day before, four gold stones for earrings, an emerald cut green stone and matching stones for earrings. The men could not hide their admiration for the stones. They picked them up with a clamp, passed them around and looked with loops.

Mr. Fair said, "You said you have others?"

Job unbuttoned his lower shirt button, opened a money belt, took out two bags and emptied them on the cloth. "That's as much as I wanted to carry on a bus from Alabama. If we strike a deal, I want weights and photographs."

"How much are you asking?"

"I know nothing about stones and values. I do know these are colored diamonds and seem to be unlike any others. You'll buy these as rocks, have them cut and sell them as something special—something no other store has. Pay me a percentage of the sales of the stones--not the mountings–just the stones."

"That is unheard of."

"Then these unheard of stones go back to Alabama. I know of no other way to set a price fair to both."

They stared at each other several minutes.

"Mr. Jobson, would you two step out for a bit?"

As they sat in the hall, they heard sounds of a phone call, a second call, then muffled words of a conversation. Ten minutes later, the door opened and they were called back. The paper on the desk had a hand written list of stone sizes and a column of prices. "Mr. Jobson, this is the best we can do. The percentages will vary according to the shape and size of the stone. We plan to cut all these. I assume you have others. After they are all cut and some mounted, we will have a big event in the spring. You are correct; they're special . . . and will be priced that way."

Job picked up the paper, looked at it and asked for a copy written and signed as a legal document. "Here is my phone number and address. When you send checks, do not let others know where I am. I don't want people digging up my yard at night. And don't call me, unless from your home. Yes, I do have other stones, but I ask you to make arrangements to pick them up to save me another bus trip. Since there will be months of delay, I want cash money to seal the deal . . . say, $10,000?"

"How many others do you have?"

"I will turn over to you twice the number you see there, more if you need them. There is one other thing. I want a gold and a green set of earrings and the emerald cut green stone mounted as a necklace. The three other gold cut stones belong to Mr. Goldstein."

"I don't think you know what you are asking for. We have had the green stones cut and the gold one reworked. They're no longer rocks."

"On the way over, Mr. Goldstein told me he wouldn't charge for cutting. The stones are mine. I ask for the mountings . . . and the money . . . and the agreement."

They stared at Job several minutes and Mr. Fair leaned across the desk and said, "I will have a document drawn up, see about the mountings and the settlement fee. It may be a while; you know the season. How should I make out the check?"

"I don't have a bank account. I will take cash."

"You want to walk the streets of this city with a bundle of money?"

"Give me packets of new hundreds and they will fit my belts. I will look a little pot-gutted and have lots of company." Two of the men glanced down.

Mr. Goldstein said, "He will not walk the street; I will take him to the station."

"Even if one of our employees walked out of the store with that much, he would carry a weapon."

"I can't carry a gun; I carry this stick. He held up a heavy twisted cane with an equally heavy transverse hand piece. "You might have noticed I don't really need it to walk." The men didn't seem to understand.

Mr. Fair said, "For cash money, it will take even longer. I have to have approval, then send a guard to the bank.

Job and the cutter left and sat in chairs outside the office. Before they were seated, Mr. Goldstein began thanking Job for the stones. "I heard Molly tell you how I cut stones all day and she never had any. She shouldn't have said that."

"Sol, I believe kindness should be returned."

When Job checked his watch the third time, his new friend said, "There is a bus this afternoon?"

"Yes, I hope to make it."

"If not, the sofa-bed is still there."

When they were called into the office, Job loaded his belt with bundles of bills and jewelry. He pulled out a smaller belt, loaded it and put it a little lower than the big belt. Some of the bills had to go in the bottom of his satchel. "With a coat, these belts won't be too noticeable. I need some sort of receipt for the jewelry and cash, in case I get searched by the cops."

They made it to the station with minutes to spare. "Mr. Goldstein said, I still can't think of words to thank you for the stones. Write down your address and phone number."

"Please remember what I told Mr. Fair and use precautions. I don't want mail or calls traced to me. Thank you for your help and kindness."

As the bus pulled away, he looked back and thought of other times he had waved to a friend he would never see again. He had to remind himself that Ima stayed in the house and didn't wave.

After hours on the first bus, Job had a late night two-hour delay for the next connection. He sat in the quiet almost deserted waiting room and tried to stay awake. In case he couldn't fight off sleep, he put his satchel between his feet and tied both handles of to one ankle. His eyes were almost closed when he saw motion a few seats over. A man opened a purse by a sleeping woman, put her billfold in his right coat pocket and came toward Job.

He thinks I am asleep. I could move and sit up, but he would run away with one billfold . . . maybe more. What should I do?

The man with bulging pockets stopped in front of Job, brought out a knife from his pocket, opened it, moved closer, and stooped down. Job did sit up to swing his stick. After the dull thud, the man dropped his knife and fell backwards into the next row of chairs with a crash and sound of breaking glass. Scattered people throughout the room jumped up. Job saw a uniform at the far end and shouted, "This drunk just fell down and broke his bottle of booze." The man lay with his head under a chair, the knife by his side and the broken bottle in his left coat pocket flooding the floor.

The officer ran up, felt the man's neck and said, "This is Willy; he makes his living in this place. He is okay and is coming around." As the crowd gathered, Job untied his satchel and walked toward a bus pulling into the loading zone. He limped and leaned on his Alabama shillelagh. As the driver got out, Job asked to be sure this was the right bus.

"Yes, we load in about ten minutes."

"Couldn't you load me now and close the door so I don't have to stand here in the cold leaning on this stick?"

"Okay, give me a ticket. That will be my present to you." Job sat low in a seat so he couldn't be seen. Several minutes later, voices woke him. He heard the officer asking people standing in line, "Have you seen a guy with a stick. I need to ask him some questions?" Job didn't sit up until the bus pulled out of the terminal.

The final bus turned into the station in late afternoon. Job leaned against the counter and asked the clerk to make a call for him.

"There's a public phone on the wall over there."

Job reached in his pocket, pulled out his change and held out his hand. In his palm were a nickel and two pennies. He didn't want to bring out a hundred for phone change.

The man behind the counter pushed his phone closer and said, "Okay, you call, but make it quick." Job called Billy Joe for a ride and asked for somebody to call Ima and tell her to put the gun away when he knocked on the door.

He did knock and say his name. He heard Ima move a chair from under the doorknob and turn the key. When the door swung open, Job saw no gun, dropped his bag and put his arms around Ima. The kiss was quick, but wet before she pushed him away and said, "I'm glad to see you, but you know we shouldn't."

He said, "You've lost weight in the few days I've been gone." He looked in the kitchen. "Most of the food I left for you is still here. Why didn't you eat?"

"I just wasn't hungry."

Job unpacked his few clothes in the bedroom and stopped by the table on Ima's side of the bed. All the envelopes were open and the pages wrinkled and worn.

Ima said, "I've read them over and over. I opened the last one today. I cried because I dreaded for tomorrow to come."

"It took longer than I expected. I'm glad to be back." Job put food in the microwave and Ima set the table. "Now let's have something to eat. I don't think I can stay awake long." Job ate, showered, and slept beyond the roll on his side of the bed almost twelve hours.

After breakfast, Job opened his money belt and took out the jewelry. "Today is Christmas day. In celebration of the birthday of one who gave the greatest gift we can imagine, we give presents to others. I have no paper to wrap this, but I brought these for you. They are made from Adam's rocks. You can wear the earrings anywhere, but the necklace with the emerald cut stone's a little dressy--but there will come a day for it." He handed her the jewelry.

"These are beautiful. What are they?"

"Diamonds--unusual diamonds, but then everything on the island was unusual."

I . . . I have nothing to give you."

"You do have. You know how I signed each letter."

She was near tears. "I can't say those words. You know why. I have the feeling, but I don't know who it's for."

"I try to understand and I know you had no way to shop. I didn't expect anything. Being here and knowing you're safe is gift enough."

"Oh, I forgot to tell you: Mr. Young called and said he is leaving town and is trying to get another attorney to take your case."

"When, how long ago? Why is he leaving?"

"He called day before yesterday. I didn't understand why he is leaving."

Job called his home. "Ben, I am sorry to bother you on Christmas day, but I just got the message about leaving. Please promise me you will do nothing until we talk. Yes, I will be there when you open at 9:30."

Job and Ima sat in the truck in front of the office on Monday at 9:25. They saw the front door unlocked at 9:30. Ben Young was standing in the empty waiting room when they opened the door. He said, "Come on in my office and sit down." Ima sat in a chair toward the corner and said nothing. "Ima told me you had taken a trip to New York. I hope it was pleasant."

"The trip was miserable, but I think effective. What is this about dropping my case?"

"I hate to admit it, but I cannot survive long enough to make it in private practice. It's a little worse now that word got out that I would handle your . . . somewhat unusual case. I will join a large group in Birmingham as soon as I can make arrangements for my clients. I have only tried on yours. I planned to give all to the same man. I got a few laughs, some unkind remarks, but no takers."

"You will be low man in a big group in a big town-- less than a secretary or low level clerk--a flunky. Is that what you want? I thought your first wish was solo practice in this town."

"My wife is my only employee, but we have to eat and pay bills. I have no choice."

Job stared at him as he rearranged papers on the desk. "I want you for my attorney. You listened to my words, took me seriously and believed me when nobody else did . . . or I thought you did. I offer you an alternative. It's a gamble, but if you win my case, your lawyer friends will be forced to admit you saw something they didn't. You saw truth when they couldn't. We can't keep it out of the paper. When word gets out, you'll have all the legal work you can do."

"That's what I had hoped, but bills have caught up."

Job stood, walked to the desk and put down bundles of bills. "I was afraid that's why you were leaving. Will four thousand cover expenses until the trial? It's probably three months away."

"How can you do this? I know you have no income."

"That was the reason for the long trip. I sold some things from the island and got a little cash."

"But how can you spend this kind of money? You have expenses too."

"In this world, there are people who pass by and never see you, but there are others. Since we came back to this country, people I never saw before have done tremendous things for us when they saw our need. Kindness and love should not be consumed and forgotten, but treasured and passed to others. I want you to win this case for me. I know it's like no other and a lot to ask."

"I don't know if I can accept this or not."

"I want you and no other to handle the case. You said nobody else would take it. Put the money in the bank. I'll be back tomorrow and we can talk about your plans for the trial."

Strange Trial

On the next morning, Ima sat in the corner and said nothing. Job and Ben Young sat at his desk and went over preparations for the trial. "Our presentation is simple. Your children had your will probated after the ship was lost and you were presumed dead. You are very much alive, although different in appearance. There is the problem. You have the log and other things from the ship to show you were on its last cruise. You have your house keys, Army dog tags, driver's license, passport, and remains of your billfold. The most important evidence is the FBI identification of your fingerprints. We'll call one of their agents and the police chief to verify all this. Then, we ask for you to be declared undead, the probating of the will nullified, and everything returned to you. Inheritance tax they've paid is another story. City, state, and federal authorities will have to be notified if we win. We could go a step further in the presentation of our case and get a DNA."

"Let's set a trap. Let them call for it."

Ben thought for a minute or so and said, "I love it; when they do, we can ask for all kinds of stipulations. Can DNA change . . . with what you have been through?"

"I don't know. To my knowledge, it never changes. It's like a set of blueprints for the production of cells through the body. My DNA makes me like I am; yours makes you like you are. In some way, mine got a new message and made younger cells, but I am the same being in a younger shell."

"But what if they don't ask for DNA?"

"Put Deoxyribonucleic acid last in our exhibit list. If their lawyer is as slow as you say, he won't know it or look it up. We can do one on me now, but we have no way to get a specimen from two years ago for comparison. If we asked for it, they would never do one now. Their agent will have to order it, when we spring the trap."

In the next few weeks, Job worked on his plants and made plans for a new greenhouse at his old home with hopes of living there again, even if with a stranger.

* * *

When the case finally began, Job managed to get in without being seen by a reporter. He asked Ima to pin up her hair under a hat, wear dark glasses, sit in the back row and speak to no one, though she never did anyway.

Ben Young's first request of the judge was to exclude the press. The judge said, "You should know, I cannot do that. There is local curiosity about this case; people see it as some sort of joke. You see how many are here on this first day. However, I will exclude photographs in the courtroom."

Mr. Young then stood and summarized the reason for the trial. "The Plaintiff alleges the Probate Court had no jurisdiction to authorize the distribution of his total assets to the Defendants. This is because the Plaintiff was then and is now alive and is the rightful owner of the assets in question. Even if Plaintiff were presumed dead, the court and Defendants did not wait the required five years. Plaintiff was not a party to the action in the Probate Court in that he was not notified of the action as required by the Alabama Rules of Civil Procedure. Plaintiff also alleges that he was prevented from appearing and defending his rights by this wrongful procedure in the Probate Court. Defendants further misinformed Plaintiff's patients by telling them their doctor was dead."

Job took the stand and told the story of the storm, the giant wave with loss of the pilothouse, crew and other passengers, and then shipwreck on the strange island. Job tried to explain why the shipwreck was far from the last known contact. He described the slow change in his body and the man who helped him. He never mentioned Ima. He offered an enlarged newspaper photograph of a young Ira Jobson Sr. to show similarity to the man on the stand. The image was blurred and unconvincing. His children would not release photographs from the past. He showed things from the ship, billfold contents and Army dog tags. Cross-examination inferred that he could have found them on a dead man lying on a beach therefore they proved nothing.

Then the opposing attorney, Mr. Sledge said, "And where is your wife to support all this wild story?"

Job knew this was coming and said, "She was lost . . . to me in the storm."

The Chief of Police from Adams County testified and presented the FBI report on the prints. The defendants' attorney asked little of the Chief, but when the FBI agent testified about the prints, he stood and took a step toward the witness. Mr. Sledge was tall and thick bodied with a fixed scowl under black hair hanging over ears and forehead. On cross-examination he seemed to tower over the witness, even in the witness box. "You have said there is almost no chance in this universe two men have the same fingerprints, but what if a set of prints were taken as a skin graft from one man and put on another? Can this be done and would the second man now have the first man's prints?"

"He would, but . . . ."

"That is all. You have answered the question; do not add commentary. Then this man claiming to be Ira Jobson could have disguised himself with new prints. I have no further questions."

From his seat, Mr. Young said, "May I redirect?"

"You may."

"Have you seen this done?"

"I have seen an attempt."

"Would you look at the plaintiff's fingers and see if you see evidence of such an attempt."

Mr. Sledge jumped up and shouted, "Objection! This witness is not a surgeon, expert in skin grafts."

Mr. Young said, "Any expert in this type surgery would be outside the law, unavailable to us and not credible if he were. This witness has seen the results of such surgery."

"Overruled. Continue."

Mr. Young said, "Please look at the plaintiffs fingers and see if you find any evidence of an attempt at change of prints as you have seen in the past."

He handed him visor loops and explained to the court the need for magnification. Job sat in an adjacent chair and the agent fitted the loops on his head and looked at each fingertip.

"I see two scars across fingertips and through the whirls of the tip that makes the print. I see nothing around the edge to suggest replacement of prints by skin graft."

The FBI witness was excused.

Mr. Sledge said, "Judge, I still object to the use of fingerprints, when the last witness testified they can be replaced. Final and true identification can only be made by DNA, which we plan to demand."

Mr. Young said, "Your honor, since defense has brought this up, I ask that we are allowed stipulations and our view of DNA results comparing specimens obtained from Dr. Jobson's past with a specimen from the Plaintiff."

"Is that agreeable to defense?"

Mr. Sledge said, "It would be if plaintiff had listed DNA on their exhibit list."

Mr. Young said, "Then you do agree, because the last item on our list is a word you probably can't pronounce and is the proper word DNA is the acronym or abbreviation for. We now call our laboratory witness."

The man was qualified and then showed a package with sealed edges and label. He testified that the package contained DNA test results from the plaintiff taken four weeks ago. The seal was to be broken at the court's direction.

"Judge, that finishes our presentation except for the DNA comparison with defense evidence which they have agreed to. We will allow their properly qualified expert to make the comparison. We obviously cannot do that until defense presents their test results taken from sources they agree is from Ira Jobson Sr."

The witness was dismissed and the Judge said, "Can defense proceed?"

After a whispered conversation with the three defendants, Mr. Sledge stood. "Plaintiff does not understand what has taken place. The will was executed because Dr. Jobson was declared dead--not presumed dead. I offer the court a copy of the Board of Inquiry findings after the ship was lost. Some bodies were recovered and the rest of the passengers and crew declared dead. We don't deny that Plaintiff is alive; we deny he is who he claims to be. We ask each child of Ira Jobson Sr. to take the stand. While they testify, they will hold a life-sized photograph of their father made a month before he left on his final cruise. Please compare the photo with the plaintiff. Body changes like Plaintiff claims have never been known in recorded history and no evidence has been presented to explain such a transformation."

Sarah testified first and loudest. She was cautioned and corrected several times about giving conclusions and not facts. She testified that the man claiming to be her father had neither the appearance nor the manor of the man she remembered. She told of the visit at the restaurant.

When the second brother stepped down, Mr. Sledge said, "None of Dr. Jobson's children recognize this Plaintiff who claims to have magically shed 50 years. Our only other presentation was to demand as final proof a DNA comparison of the plaintiff to that of the real Dr. Jobson. We were not aware that DNA had been obtained on the Plaintiff and would be presented. For us to get tests on the real Ira Jobson Sr. we will have a delay of several days to get the laboratory results."

Mr. Young tried to hide his smile and said, "We have our DNA test ready now for comparison. You have seen the sealed package containing the results. Since defendants have agreed to our stipulations, with court appointed supervision for verification, we ask that samples be taken from several sources to be certain of identification of the man all agree to be Ira Jobson Sr. Apparently his office has remained empty. We suggest the pen at his desk and the place his hands rested on the arms of the chair where he sat. If those are not the same, use the handle of his old cane. We ask that defense expert bring his sealed findings, as our expert did, open the packages and compare the two on the stand. You must have no prior communications."

Mr. Sledge said, "This routine is unheard of."

Ben Young said," This case is unheard of. It calls for unheard of procedures."

The judge said, "Mr. Sledge why did you not obtain the DNA results before the trial. You risk declaration of a mistrial."

"We assumed it would take several days to have plaintiff's DNA done at our request. We did not know it had been done."

The judge said, "Never assume anything. We adjourn for one week. Get the results by a lab acceptable to plaintiff. Be here then and we'll settle this."

The week seemed more like a year. When the trial began again, defendant's laboratory representative was called to the stand and his expertise established. He held a sealed packet. "These are labeled as the results from specimens taken from objects in Dr. Ira Jobson's office: his pen, the arms of his chair and his old cane. I personally took and evaluated the specimens. All these patterns are the same."

Mr. Young called their own expert and reminded the court of his qualifications. He handed defense's lab expert the packet of the test results taken from Job, five weeks before. Mr. Sledge said. "Sir, please tell us if the plaintiff--the man sitting there--could possibly be the same one who sat in Dr. Jobson's chair."

The lab expert wiped his brow and stammered his answer. "I can open the packages and compare the patterns now--visually. It will take quite a while. I can give a more accurate answer by using the computers in our lab."

The judge glared at both attorneys and said, "Do so, but this is the last delay we will allow. The court will send a reprehensive who will be responsible for the packages at all times until we reconvene."

When the court began again, the deputy testified about the security of the packages and the lab expert took the stand. Mr. Sledge said, "Sir, do you remember the question I asked you?

The witness looked down at the packages—one in each hand. The courtroom was so quiet, when a man in the back sneezed, every person jumped as if a cannon had been fired. He put one package on the other and looked up. "Yes sir. All the patterns in these two packages are the same. They are from the same person."

Mr. Sledge jumped up. "Sir, is it possible in some fashion to change DNA?"

He hesitated then said, "Yes . . . ."

Mr. Sledge held up his hand and sat down.

Mr. Young said, "Judge, since part of this is our evidence, may I speak? May I question the defense witness?"

"You may."

"Tell us about this change."

"It is a very complicated time consuming process few can do."

"In your opinion, could a man trained as a surgeon do this to himself?"

"No, few in this country could. He would need others to help, a laboratory and chemicals."

After the witness was excused, the attorneys gave their closing arguments. The judge said, "Court will reconvene Monday. I will render a decision then."

The courtroom was full on Monday. Out of town reporters were in the front row. Sketches of Job's face compared with the photographs had already made the back pages of some big city newspapers as one of the ridiculous events of the South. As the judge sat, he did not appear to consider the event a joke.

"The court is called on for Declaratory Judgment. Plaintiff vs. the three children of Ira Lee Jobson Sr.: Sara Eve Jackson, Ira Lee Jobson Jr., and Joshua Lee Jobson. Plaintiff claims he is their father, Ira Lee Jobson Sr., a man who all agree appears 50 years younger than his chronological age of 83. He claims his will was wrongly executed while he was alive. Plaintiff presented personal items and objects from the cruise ship that all agree Ira Jobson Sr. was on when it was lost in a storm and all persons on the ship declared dead.

Plaintiff testified as to the shipwreck in the storm and the change he underwent while he lived on an island for the next year

A communication from the FBI offered as evidence and verified by an agent, identified Plaintiff's fingerprints as those of Ira Lee Jobson Sr. Defense claimed alteration of prints, but there was no evidence or testimony to support such a change. Plaintiff 's laboratory expert presented sealed DNA readings taken from the plaintiff. Defendants agreed to later comparison with DNA patterns from the office of Dr. Ira Jobson Sr.

Each defendant testified that plaintiff was not the man they remember as their father. This was further demonstrated by comparison of a photograph of their father taken just before his cruise with the appearance of the Plaintiff. Defense argues that if a man doesn't look the age of the man remembered, he is not that man. Defense further argues that children recognize their own father.

Defendants presented DNA from items in the medical office of Dr. Ira Jobson, which had been unused for two years. According to prior stipulation, Defense's expert in the field compared the DNA evidence from the Plaintiff with the DNA evidence from items in the office of Ira Jobson Sr. and said they were identical; therefore, all were from the same person.

The Defendants deny Plaintiff as their father. However, the Court cannot disregard fingerprint evidence from the FBI and the scientific DNA identification verified by defense's own witness. The Court is acutely aware that forces have been at work that we do not comprehend, but finds for the Plaintiff."

As soon as Ben Young could control his smile, he stood and presented his proposed finding and court order. As he handed the sheets he said, "I am sure the court appreciates the strange circumstances of this case. I believe my recommendations are reasonable and follow what little precedent there is. I ask that my client's life and remaining possessions be restored and improperly collected taxes returned."

He sat as the judge adjourned the court. Job said, "Do I have my life, house, and office back now?"

Ben said, "The will is voided. They may appeal, but as weird as this is, I don't think a higher court will touch it."

"Then get us out of here by a back way. I am afraid of what might happen."

They stopped at Ben's office; Job made the call to the locksmith and emphasized the urgency of the call. He called the Sheriff's office and twisted the truth slightly. He asked Ben to watch his old office. Mr. Young warned that he was moving too fast. Job and Ima drove to the home. A deputy's car was just behind them. Three cars were parked in front of the house. Two appeared to be new. As Job walked toward the house, his son-in- law came out of the open doorway carrying two small paintings. Ira Jr. came behind carrying a bronze. Josh was closing the door of his car.

Sarah stopped in the doorway. She said, " I don't care what that judge said; you are not the father we knew. We are taking what's ours."

Job said, "The law sees it a little differently. Deputy, I want this written up, maybe breaking and entering. I'm not going to press charges, but I want it on record."

They put the paintings and bronze back. Josh brought things from his car as far as the porch. They gave information to the deputy and left. Josh drove through a flowerbed. The locksmith came and changed the keys on all doors.

They drove to the office. Ben Young was in his car in the parking lot. He opened the door and said, "A car came by and I thought they were turning in, but they didn't. Couldn't tell who it was. I hope you didn't do anything that will cause problems." The office locks were changed.

When Job closed the door on their little house, Ima said, "Then it's all over. You have your life back?"

"I wish it were true. It's the beginning, but now there is a way, if our finances hold out."

Two days later, Job faxed court documents to his stockbroker, then called and convinced him that he was still alive. He was almost sorry he called; much of his funds had been withdrawn and stocks sold.

* * *

He made another bus trip. The trip to Atlanta was much shorter. He took copies of the court records and the fingerprint document. He got the expected response of, "But our records show you would be 83. Liability coverage was closed out 18 months ago when we got a letter saying Dr. Ira Jobson was dead."

"The man before you is obviously not dead. I'm here to see if you will cover me again. I have been inactive for two years and plan to take a mini- residency, when I can convince some place to take me at age 83. I will need coverage as of that date. You might even get a little free advertisement out of it."

After repeating the story several times, Job got his agreement of coverage in writing. He would pay a week before the effective date. He didn't have the money anyway.

The next step was to write letters to medical organizations, governmental organizations, and others to announce that he was declared undead by the courts. He hired a retired secretary part time to do the letters. He had a hard time getting a new driver's license. He had to wait for a new worker who didn't notice the age.

He began construction of a greenhouse connected to his real home. He avoided much time in the house. He was depressed by the empty spaces.

One day, a letter arrived with a strange return address in New York. There was also a package with a different address. The letter had a check and a handwritten note: *We had a great opening. Here is a list of what we sold.* The packet had a list and photographs of stones cut and a note: *My wife is wearing the stones. Thank you again.*

Now he could finish the greenhouse, clean up the house, and move in, after being away two years. Ima was no different and still would not agree to any medical studies and evaluation.

Final Move
They moved the plants into the new greenhouse. Billy Joe helped and smiled when Job told him to set up the old empty greenhouse for flowers. Fog and sprinklers were automatic in the new greenhouse. There were alarms in the house and a generator in case of power failure. Job and Ima packed their clothes and drove to the house that had been home to Job, but was a strange building to Ima.

They went through the rooms and Job told Ima about the furnishings. She said, "Everything is so fresh and clean—not like it had been closed up for so long."

"I called the lady who was part time housekeeper. She cleaned up two years of dust." Last of all, they walked toward the large bedroom. "Ima, this house has other bedrooms; you've seen them. You can have your own room if you want. You could even have this one and I would take one of the small ones."

"No, I need to know you are close by. Our sleeping arrangements are fine. I know you had to go, but I had a terrible time when you were in New York."

As they got to the entrance to the bedroom, Ima stopped, took a hesitant step, seemed to stumble, and fell against the wall. She would have fallen to the floor if Job had not caught her.

"What's wrong?"

Her mouth was open; she looked unconscious. Job held her upright. She was limp and made no effort to stand.

"Ima--Ima, what's wrong? Did you hit your head again? It couldn't have been that hard. Ima wake up!" He was dragging her over to the bed when she jerked spasmodically, straightened up, pulled away and sat on the bed. She took quick short breaths that gradually slowed. After several minutes of silence, she looked up.

"I'm fine now. I just had some . . . some kind of spell, but it's passed. I've . . . uh . . . seen the house, now I need to go to the . . . is there a shopping mall close by? I need to buy something."

"There is one a few miles down the road."

"Could you give me some money and let me use the truck?"

"You haven't driven in two years. I know how hard it was for me after a year. I'll drive you."

"But you can't come in."

As they sat in the truck, Job gave her two bills. "Put these in your pocket, I don't know what you want. Will $150 be enough?" She nodded. Ima stared straight ahead and said nothing during the ride. He let her off at the entrance to the mall. "I'll watch this door and drive by as soon as you come out. If I don't see you in a half hour, I *am* coming in."

She was back in 20 minutes, carrying a small pink package. If there was a label, she covered it with her arm. She looked straight ahead and said nothing.

After supper, they watched TV for an hour. Job said, "Are you sure you wouldn't like your own bedroom? I would still be in the house."

"No, if you show me where the extra bedding is, I will fix the roll between us, while you have the bathroom."

"You know there are other bathrooms."

"This one is fine; I don't mind waiting a few minutes."

Job showered and dressed for bed. He stared at the shaving kit he had not unpacked, picked up a bottle and shook it. There were a few sleeping pills left. For the first time in two years he was about to go to bed with his wife in his own house, but she didn't know she was his wife. He would sleep on his side of the dividing roll and hear her breathe, but couldn't touch her. He took a pill from the bottle, looked at it in his hand, then carried it to the bedroom and put it on the bedside table.

He called to Ima, "Your time."

She left the door partly open as she always did. After her shower, she took a little longer than usual dressing for bed. Job tried to ignore the sounds, put his back against the dividing roll and lay on his right side facing the wall so he wouldn't see her when she came to bed. He left the lights on so she could see in the unfamiliar room. He checked the location of the sleeping pill so he could find it in the dark.

He heard shuffling steps, and then they stopped. "My name is *not* Ima Who . . . *I* am Lisa . . ."

Job jerked around and was on his elbows in an instant. She had taken another step and was pulling back the covers.

"I am back . . . and *I* belong to you . . . and *you* Job, belong to me."

Beneath the smile she wore the green diamond necklace. Below that, two strips of clothing covered the essentials, but barely. He knew that pink bag had come from Elizabeth's Secret. She leaned over, the smile widened, the stone swung from her neck as she pulled away the dividing roll. "Your mouth is open, but you're not saying anything and not moving. You need help with that jammie-top?"

Job regretted his cool shower, but not for long.

At the table the next morning, Lisa wore Ima's modest robe. Job could hardly eat for Lisa holding and rubbing his hand. After he gave up on breakfast, he said, "I told you there would come a day for that necklace. I think it fitting for your return. Did everything come back in a flood when you almost fell?"

"I thought some was coming back when we went through the rest of the house, but when we went toward the bedroom, all the memories did wash over me like a flood. Now, I don't remember everything about Ima. I would like to forget it all. I don't see how you endured her."

"I knew you were there, somewhere inside. It was hard to wait until Lisa came back."

She said, "Now I understand why Ima wanted you in sight all the time. As Ima, I felt the pain of separation, but didn't know why. You were my only connection with reality, but I didn't realize it. Now that we are home, what will you do with the fruit? The world would probably pay a fortune for them."

"I don't think there are enough special greenhouses in the country to grow the orange and yellow ones for food. If you remember what I told you when you were Ima, we must never mention the wrinkled brown fruit. If we did, a mob would demolish this place to find them. Even if we could grow enough to feed the whole country, think what would happen: people on every square foot. There wouldn't be enough oxygen to breathe. Then the rest of the world would be after them. We have to decide what to do. We still eat the dried brown fruit. Should we keep them for ourselves? Is this some sort of transgression for us? Suppose those old guys in the Bible lived so long after the garden account because they ate the fruit? If so, they must have lost it a few generations after the flood when their lives were shorter. Are we obligated to destroy the plants and fruit we brought? Should we keep them in reserve, but stop eating the fruit like Adam did, with the thought there might be an urgent need some day? For now, I'm growing the plants, but answers are complicated."

He watched Lisa as she considered these matters. "It is a problem, but don't frown like that. Smile; I like to see it and I haven't seen you smile in two years." He reached out to her. "I like that stone, too . . . and where it lies."

"Job, you're checking below the stone . . . a lot lower. I have come back after two years. We're young again, our love is greater, but we'll never catch up."

"We left for a pleasure cruise that took us across land and sea. We survived two storms, a shipwreck, and a year on a strange island; we got our youth back; we sailed the Pacific in a little boat, lived through a tsunami, and crossed the country in a truck. I rode the bus to a strange city in the dead of winter. We sued our own children to get our lives back. One day, we will get them back. We can now call Ezra. Most people would say we have done the impossible."

Job held her hand and stood. "You may be right about catching up, but now that the barrier roll is gone, we can try."

Afterward

Job changed his mind about his practice. In the last few years, surgeons had begun operating through long tubes and with robots. There were a thousand strange new tests, studies, and drugs. Sometimes, it seemed that doctors treated tests and not patients. His body was young, but he couldn't quit the past. He couldn't operate without feeling tissues with his fingers. In years gone by, after he had done a two-layer hook-up of bowel, he could feel the opening and check for leaks.

He took a mini-residency in dermatologic surgery. Anything he operated on, he could see and touch. The hospital that finally accepted him as a joke had trouble believing he was 83 years old and was even more surprised to discover what he already knew and could do. He felt more at home in this type surgery. When he finished, he went back home, hired an office crew, and put an announcement of his practice in the paper--with a new picture and one from the time of the cruise. Some came out of curiosity, some thought Job could make them young, but they came and his office was busy the first day. Even after the first day, they kept coming. Ben Young was just as busy. Job didn't have to work. Billy Joe was doing well with the greenhouse business and more checks came from New York. Job refused requests from the geriatric experts for "tests and studies."

Lisa and Job filled the mails with birthday cards, anniversary cards and letters. After more than a year, both sons showed up at their door. After long discussions and a few tears, Ira Jr. and Josh believed and accepted this strange situation. Their noisy sister, her husband, and children moved without a forwarding address--neighbors thought to somewhere in Oregon.

As the sons drove away, Lisa said, "We must look on the positive side; we have two out of three; a year ago we had none." After one of her sly smiles she said, "We can keep trying to reach her, but we might decide to replace that daughter."

Job said, "You don't mean having a baby at 80?"

"The Bible says Sarah had one at 90. Maybe Abraham fed her the wrinkled brown fruit, way back then. We don't know how long it's been around."

They made the greenhouse secure with steel bars, alarms, and electric fences. They kept the plants that bore pink fruit--dried wrinkled brown and so changed their lives. Job hid them in the center of all the others. They ate ordinary food like others, but after their trees matured, on many days they had nothing but fruits they had eaten for a year on the island. The glow returned to Lisa's cheeks. They ate the brown fruit less frequently so they would age, but at a slower rate than others.

One night, Lisa was slow in the bathroom and left the darkness of the hall with shuffling steps wearing two thin strips and a smile. She said, "I'm still Lisa."

Job suddenly sat up. Lisa had made anther trip to Elisabeth's Secret. Job said, "You were Ima beyond the roll for two years. What about the years we dated and were forced to delay our beginning? Let's go back to every day on that brown fruit; we need more time to catch up."

About the Names

Job—A whole book in the bible is devoted to him. He had his troubles, but came out well

Amnon—David's first son. He raped his sister and was killed by his brother.

Cain—Adam's bad son

Bildad—The first of Job's advisors

David—A good man, but he had his problems

Adam—The first man

www.ingramcontent.com/pod-product-compliance
Lightning Source LLC
Chambersburg PA
CBHW051143020726
47501CB00005B/1657